first edition

 Canada Council **Conseil des Arts** for the Arts du Canada  ONTARIO ARTS COUNCIL CONSEIL DES ARTS DE L'ONTARIO Canadä

Published with the generous assistance of the Canada Council for the Arts and the Ontario Arts Council. Coach House Books also acknowledges the support o the Government of Ontario through the Ontario Book Publishing Tax Credit and the Government of Canada through the Book Publishing Industry Development Program.

LIBRARY AND ARCHIVES CANADA CATALOGUING IN PUBLICATION

Blouin, Michael, 1960-
    Chase and Haven / Michael Blouin.

ISBN 978-1-55245-203-5
    I. Title.

PS8603.L69C43 2008   C813'.6   C2008-905599-3

this one's for my father,
the anti-Jack,
thanks for waiting

and for Deborah, with love and squalor

'thus you write a history
use words you've used before
your own voice speaking in the morning whispering'
– bpNichol, *The Martyrology*

'It's a hard world for little things.'
– Robert Mitchum, *The Night of the Hunter*

Dawn

The red start of the morning.

This will happen, if it happens at all, for the same reason that all things happen: because they are inevitable. It's 9:30 in the morning and it's the middle of the bottle.

Happen.

Chase sat in the Jeep for a while and looked out over the now shining lake. Fingertips along the wheel. Two black crows arguing about something in the pine trees. Dew on the hood. Thirty-seven years old. The time to think. A little time. When the frogs died all over the lawn, and when they ran from their parents and when Mary's grandfather died they kept him in a pine box on the porch for two months until the ground was warm enough to dig a hole to put him in. He might have another drink. Probably not. He probably shouldn't bother having another drink now. Haven wouldn't want to see that in the toxicology report. That's what that was called. Maybe that. Or something else like that. How many drinks did it take to show up? Probably too late.

Now.

Like putting on a sweater and taking it off because it didn't fit well. It was the right thing to do. Haven was always right about things. Right about everything. She always knew what to do. She wouldn't do this. But she wasn't living this life, holding everything against the dark.

Watched Lucky chasing around the campsite, running from one Oh Henry! wrapper to the next, back and forth and barking at the yellow paper. They'd find Lucky okay. He shouldn't worry about that. He could stop that. Stop now.

Now.

Waited.

Didn't think about his father. Never thought about his father. But he thought about the train, how when the train came the whole world just shook. How it shook under his feet. No, stop. Just stopstopstop. Just wanted to lie down for a while. Wake up rested and get this done in a pure way.

Simply.

He was right to do what he was doing. It was the thing that should be done. That's all. So he set about doing it.

Because it was inevitable.

The thing that should be done.

Do it.

Chase looked out over the lake again. Put the handbrake on. Got out of the Jeep and gathered the things he would need. No other way out. The dry crunch of leaves. Went to tie up Lucky.

One

*These are the things that took place
in the morning with the return of the sun*

'You know what I do, Grandma?' April asked.

There was still early frost on the windshield. Mary had brought April with her so Haven could get some sleep after being up all night with her medical books. Haven needed rest. April needed some mothering. And groceries. Everyone needed groceries.

'What's that, my darlin'?' Mary answered through the rear-view mirror.

'I squinch up my eyes … like this … like this, Grandma.'

'I'm looking.'

'And then I open them and there's all these little stars swimming and falling down.'

'Yes, well, that's okay.'

'And I pretend God's coming … '

'That's nice, darlin' … '

We all pretend that, sweetie, Mary thought, pulling into the parking lot. *We all do that.*

She bought four bags of cookies with April's help. They weren't on the list, but the world could always use more cookies. When your father ups and leaves you for no good reason, an extra cookie won't hurt. Be cheaper to make 'em, but April liked her Oreos and Chips Ahoy! Mr. Christie, you make good cookies. She wondered at the world. Chase and Haven ending up on her doorstep years ago. Her never thinking she'd have children and then suddenly those two. Bringing them up as best she could. Like they were hers, and they were, and now Haven's little one. She helped April sort the bags of cookies in the cart. Her little fingers. And herself, she thought, plain amongst the women. This week she would keep on packing the lunches, keep on dusting and sweeping and doing all of the work that continued the world.

&

When Haven was little, before going to live with Mary, before marriage, and before April, before the end of marriage, before everything became too real on cold winter mornings, she would lie in on spring mornings in the growing warmth, and in the summer with the sun lighting up the thin bare wood panelling of the trailer, and would float up as if she were pulled by a long cord from the sky and she would rise up through the thin roof, the pink insulation and the shingles, hover over the small yard and leaning woodshed, up past the trees and above the highway and the black roads and the Kemptville creek, the tiny cars and people moving slowly down streets and sidewalks past the small houses and shops. The air blew through the bathrobe she wore to bed, lifting it away from her body, and she could stretch through the lazy sky beneath her as if it were a blanket.

&

'Has it ever occurred to you that we're grown-ups now?' Haven asked him once.

'No,' Chase said. It hadn't.

They met for coffee in different places. This was way before the Tim Horton's opened up. Mostly they met at the Bright Star and watched the cars go by the window. People doing their errands.

'You know those inappropriate thoughts that go through your head?' he asked her.

'Which ones?'

'Any of them. Things you don't want to think about. You know, thoughts that, really, you shouldn't think – that you wouldn't, like, you wouldn't want to share them with anyone.'

'Sure.'

'You have those?'

'Sure.'

Chase poured another sugar into his coffee.

'I'm not telling you what they are,' she said.

'No, it's just, well, how often do you have those?' he asked her. He picked up his spoon and turned it around his cup.

Haven looked at him. 'Once in a while … ' she said. 'You?'

Chase made himself laugh and tossed the empty sugar packet into the garbage by the waitress station.

'It's the only kind I have,' he said and made himself keep laughing and she laughed with him then and it was okay and they picked up their menus and ordered some breakfast.

But it was mostly true.

And he thought that probably she knew that it was mostly true but he didn't want to go any further than that. And she didn't ask him to.

'Do you ever think about when we were kids?' she asked him.

&

Haven found Chase's other boot behind the couch next to the cat.

'Hurry up, you two, I will not be late walking into church.'

They never went to church but it was Easter and she had been up all night cooking and whatever else she did all night when she was like this. She had pulled them both out of bed and told them to hurry and get dressed.

'The worst kind of people on earth are late for church.'

Everything was melting outside. There was a puddle of water on the floor near the door.

'I will not walk into church late on Easter of all days.'

Easter was pretty much the only day they ever walked into church.

'The worst kind of people on earth, the lowest of the low, and that is not us. Jack, get those eggs done like I said so they'll be ready by the time we get home.'

Their father was apparently not going to church. Their mother had the car keys in her hand, shaking them like the house was on fire.

'C'mon, Chase, it does not take this long to get a pair of boots on,' she said.

Their father was watching a fishing show.

'You know what to do now, Jack, with the eggs,' she was calling to him.

'Colour the eggs,' he said, his eyes still on the TV.

'Dye the eggs,' she said as if she were explaining it for the third or fourth time, which she probably was.

'Right. Dye … the … eggs … ' he repeated slowly.

It was time to go, Haven knew, time to get them separated.

'We're ready, Mom,' she said.

She had Chase by the door. Their boots were on, coats and hats.

Now her mother was doing something at the oven.

'And this cake has to be taken out in exactly twenty minutes or it won't be any good.'

'Dye … the … eggs … ' he said again from the couch, a little louder this time with bigger spaces between the words.

'Okay, we're ready to go, Mom,' Haven said.

She was looking around the kitchen like she'd forgotten something.

'Mom?'

'Okay,' she said and then she turned and came toward them quickly, opening the door and shovelling them out in one motion.

'The eggs, Jack, and the cake,' she called back into the trailer.

'DYE … THE … ' You could still hear the word *eggs* muffled after she closed the door.

When they got back from church, Haven made sure she was through the door first. Her dad was not on the couch and the eggs were just where Haven was afraid they'd be – still in the carton on the counter. They weren't coloured, but he had written on each one of them with a pencil and a marker: *Happy Fucking Easter, Happy Fucking Easter, Happy Fucking Easter*.

'C'mon,' she said to Chase.

He was still looking at the eggs.

'C'mon,' she said and she took his hand and pulled him down the hall.

Their father was coming out of the bathroom. The sound of the toilet behind him.

'How was church?' he asked. He was wiping his hands on his pants.

'Good,' she said.

She kept them moving quick towards the bedroom. She got the door closed just as she heard their mother come in and drop the two boxes of mashed potatoes she'd bought on the way home onto the counter.

It was quiet.

'What?' Chase asked.

She waited.

Then they listened as the eggs hit what sounded like the kitchen cupboards one at a time and their father yelled out things like 'Hey!' and 'What the hell?' and 'They're decorated for Chrissake, willya stop?'

1
2
3
4
5
6

7
8
9
10
11

12

Haven counted to herself.

'You can take off your coat now,' she told Chase.

She had a box of things she liked to take out when no one was around. Crayons. A watch. Safety pin. Pennies. A marble. A pencil. Jacks. Two little dolls Chase had found once. She loved to draw pictures of birds.

They were driving a long way. Chase was wishing for his eighth birthday and what he wanted was a radio. He was sitting in the front seat of the station wagon and resting his head against the window. He lifted his feet when they went over train tracks. He counted mailboxes but there were too many of them and then they were in the city and there weren't any. His father smoked cigarettes and listened to the radio. The news. Music. They went over the big bridge to Hull and Chase held his breath for as long as he could so he wouldn't smell the smoke from the mill. They made paper there. He didn't know why making paper would stink so much.

His father swore a few times driving up and down little streets looking for the address. He kept looking at the dashboard and swearing at it too.

'When you grow up, Chase, you get a good job, and a good car,' he said.

Chase said that he would.

'Then you can drive me around,' his father said, squinting again at a piece of paper that had the address on it. 'If I'm not dead.'

They turned another corner.

'Yes!' his father exclaimed, looking at a little house with painted white wood and blue shutters. It was on a hill street crowded with little houses like it.

There was a couch sitting on the front lawn.

'There we go,' his father said and he pulled on the emergency brake and got out of the car with the engine running.

He never turned off the engine if he didn't have to because sometimes the car didn't start again. Unless they were in their own driveway and then it was safe. There was a cardboard pine tree hanging from the rear-view mirror that was supposed to smell but it didn't have any smell on it anymore. You could scratch it even and all that happened was the green ink got under your fingernail. Chase got out of the car. His father was at the top of the little concrete steps at the front door ringing the doorbell.

Chase stood looking at the couch. It had glass ashtrays stuck in the arms.

'Nobody home,' his father said, coming back down the little steps. There were little metal railings on either side of the steps and one side was loose and leaning.

Right then the car shuddered and stopped.

'Shit,' his father said and ran to the car and jumped in to start it again. Sometimes if he started it again right away it would go. It didn't go.

'Shit shit shit shit sonofabitch,' his father yelled, slamming his hands against the steering wheel.

He sat there for a while and then he got out again and slammed the door hard twice. He walked over to where Chase was standing and looked at the couch. He stayed looking at the couch for a while.

'Look at those ashtrays,' he said.

'I know,' Chase said, 'they're cool.'

His father stood looking at the couch still and then he took out his cigarettes and lit one. He walked around the back of the couch looking at it and then sat down at one end and tapped his cigarette into one of the ashtrays. Then he sat looking out into the street.

Chase sat down next to him. His father got back up and tried the car once more but it didn't go. He didn't swear this time and he left the radio playing and then he got back out. He sat back down on the couch and they listened to the music. It had started to rain.

&

Chase started to write his first novel at the age of twelve. Just a couple of years after they ran from their parents and ended up with Mary. And many years before the campsite. Before the bear.

'I'm writing a book,' he told Mary over oatmeal.

'Y'cn barely read,' she said.

'I'm writing a book,' he insisted.

'Fine then. Just don't trouble me with it,' she relented. 'Just leave me out of it or I'll smack you.'

She didn't mean it, though, and that was the difference with Mary – first she told him she would hit him, and then she never did. When she was mad she just gave him the look. And sometimes she hugged him very tight.

'You're the star of it,' he told her.

21

She gave him the look. That book never came to anything more than a page, but when he was twenty-one he self-published a book of short stories and brought it to her.

'I wrote it,' he told her.

'You did what?'

'I wrote this book.'

'You never did.' She took the book from him and held it at arm's length as if it might jump at her. 'It's got your name on it ... What's in it?'

'Stories.'

She looked at him. 'What, out of your head like?'

'Yeah.'

'Like, lies? Stuff you made up that's not true?'

Chase thought about it. 'I guess that's right.'

She looked at it more closely for a minute. 'And they pay you for that?'

'Yeah. Well, when people buy it.'

She put the book down. 'Right. Well, that's good then.'

She studied the cover again. 'A cup of tea wouldn't be a terrible thing. Are you just gonna stand there in the hopes that the tea'll brew itself?'

&

Lonely. Making up the bed with the flap of crisp white sheets. Her breasts hanging pale in the long mirror screwed to the back of the closet door. White, and lonely.

'Children wear you down,' her mother once told Haven. 'Everything wears you down, till there's nothing left.'

No sense wishing you were born to something better. You get what you get.

&

Afraid. That's what he was.

'Listen, April,' he said.

He'd brought her to the Bright Star for breakfast. Haven had to work, so he picked up April and drove her to school.

'What is it?' she asked. She knew it was something. She was like Haven.

'What's Grade 10 like now?' Chase asked her.

She smiled. 'It's okay, my friends are pretty cool. Some of the teachers are okay … '

Chase ordered pancakes. He never had pancakes there. He was doing more of that lately – doing things he didn't usually do.

'Pretty cool … ' he echoed.

'What?'

'Your friends, they're pretty cool?'

'Oh, yeah, we have a great time. We're pretty tight, you know?'

'Yeah.' Chase poured his syrup.

He thought about himself in Grade 10. He'd spent most of high school learning about drinking.

This wasn't how he'd thought this out. Never mind. She probably knew anyway.

'You're not eating your eggs,' he said.

'What? Oh yeah … '

That he loved her.

&

The cracking of the radiator, the smell of Ivy's perfume, cold cream, fried eggs, toast, lemon soap, strong coffee. Ivy. All the smells all at once, all awash with them. Like somebody talking too fast. It was him. The patterns in his head.

23

Cigarette smoke. Candy. Sport bra. Lipstick. A smell of the colour yellow.

Late slanting sun through the windows. He turned again in the sheets.

What if I just tell her?

Now.

Chase looked down at his toes resting in a pool of sunlight cast by the blinds. He felt disconnected from them and from the rest of his body as if he were tethered by small ropes like a balloon. Next to him, Ivy's body rose and fell steadily with her breath. He lifted his hand gently and slowly from the sheets, little balloons lifting his hand and resting it on her shoulder. On the slope of her waist where it met her hip. There. Warm.

'It was like this,' he told her.

Her open face and her jagged black hair shining. Her jagged black hair.

He told her about the Christmases, about the birthday parties, about the calls from the school, about the police, he told her about the pig, he told her about the guns, about Haven almost dying, about how they ran away then and ended up with Mary. He didn't tell her about the train. He didn't tell her everything. Never told anyone everything, not even Haven.

'Like this … ' And he told her about it, her dark eyes wider.

'Well,' she said finally when he was finished telling her his childhood, her hands lightly tracing the black hair from her eyes and then falling like small nesting birds between her legs. She was always in her underwear. White cotton underwear and her legs long and dark. A T-shirt, blue or green. Her courier bike rested against the wall in the bedroom.

'Well … ' she said again, tucking one leg beneath her on the bed and looking at him.

She smelled like lemons. The skin tight across her forehead.

Like oranges or limes. Citrus. Drank wine through a straw. The T-shirt cotton stretched across her. Each evening she'd wash the city from her body, standing in the shower for a full half-hour, and in the morning she'd go out and begin to apply it again. On Saturday she'd stay in bed, then make hot chocolate, standing in the steam from the stove. There were no envelopes to deliver on Saturdays. He'd watch her as she shaved her legs. Kiss her on the smooth skin. He had the first dreams he'd ever remembered having.

His hands after they made love, full of the smell of her. The taste.

Her skin light brown, like velvet, coffee, the soles of her feet like paper.

He lay still and studied the angles of the room. Pictured the surfaces of the bricks outside the window in the February light, the cold flat of their surfaces. The frozen iron of the fire escape. The grey-streaked glass of the window, which had hidden how many others from the winter dawns.

Having and keeping. Two different things.

I am very still, he thought. *I am not moving.*

There was nothing to do and they'd been driving since breakfast, which was toast without butter since there was no butter. Chase was playing a game where he pretended his hand was an airplane and he held it out the window and let the wind carry it up or down. The sun was gleaming off the chrome trim around the window. You could move your hand like the flaps on a plane's wing and your hand would lift up or go down. Sometimes you'd lose control of it and you'd have to go on the speaker and apologize to the passengers for the turbulence. He got tired of flying and opened the glove compartment to see if there was anything new in it.

Sitting there unopened was a box of Glosettes chocolate-covered peanuts. Once their mother had made their father stop at the Hershey plant in Smiths Falls and they had gone on a tour and they each got a box of Glosettes for free. This was a new one, though. Chase looked up to see if his dad had seen him open the glove compartment. His dad was looking right at him.

'Go ahead,' he said, 'you can have it.'

He was smiling.

It was a snow day. There were no buses. Other kids cheered when there was a snow day. They got up early in the morning to listen to the radio for the announcement. They talked about it at recess the day before.

'It's gonna be one for sure.'

'On the radio they said ten inches and freezing rain.'

'No way buses are gonna go through that.'

And they stood around like they were congratulating each other on winning some award or something. For Haven it just meant working harder.

'Finish those up and let's get going,' her father said.

Haven looked down at her Eggos. Chase was watching from behind the toaster. *What do you want me to do,* he was asking, *what should I do?*

He came back into the room with a BB pistol. They had never seen it before except on the shelf in Canadian Tire. She knew what it was because Chase had told her all about it. He had asked for it for Christmas.

'Let's go,' her father said and she got up and put on her coat and boots.

She didn't look back at Chase. He was safe. He had his Eggos and syrup.

When they opened the door, the cat bolted in past them.

'Just 'cause a girl's a girl doesn't mean she shouldn't know how to shoot a gun,' her father said when they were standing in the little yard behind the trailer.

He took a little tin out of his coat pocket and unscrewed the lid. Inside it were the little metal bullets. She didn't know if they were called bullets or not.

'Here, hold these,' he said, handing the tin to her.

Then he took out his pack of Players and lit one. 'Nice day,' he said.

The freezing rain had stopped but now it was snowing pretty hard. If they were at school it would be time to put away the spelling books and do math. They were doing areas of rectangles. It was easy.

He reached into the tin for a bullet. It dropped onto the frozen snow, rattling around on the smooth surface and dropping into a footprint.

'Shit,' he said from around his cigarette and he reached for another. She held the tin tight and still. Her fingers were cold on the metal.

'There we go.'

He flipped out a little holder on the side of the gun and slipped one of the little bullets into it carefully and then closed it up again with his thumb. Then he pulled a lever on the bottom of the gun and cranked it back into place. He was cocking the gun, she knew that from Chase and from hearing it in western movies. That's what it meant when people said, 'Don't go off half-cocked' – it meant that you couldn't shoot right.

'What do you want to kill?' he asked her and he looked around the yard.

Haven was still holding the tin in front of her like she was collecting for charity.

'Give me that,' he said.

He handed her the gun and she took it, careful not to look scared of it. He showed her how to hold it, his big hands wrapped around hers. She kept it pointed at the ground.

'How about one of those Beefaroni cans?' he asked, pointing to a spilled garbage bag by the lean-to. 'Looks like the 'coons are done with 'em.'

He crunched with his boots through the frozen snow and picked one up and set it on top of the overturned garbage pail. He turned back to Haven and then turned the can so *Beefaroni* was facing out.

'Go ahead,' he called, 'take a bead on it … '

Haven lifted up the gun like she'd seen people do on *Mannix*. She stared down the top of the barrel and tried to make sure that her hands didn't shake. Snowflakes were landing on the black metal and melting. She waited for him to move away. She pretended to be lining up her shot while she waited. It didn't look like he was going to move. Then he did.

'Try not to shoot me in the ass!' he said.

She steadied the gun again. She had no idea if she'd be able to hit the can. She thought probably she wouldn't. She decided at the last second that it would be safer not to hit it and she jerked her hands a bit to make sure as she pulled the trigger. There was a popping sound and the can didn't move. She couldn't tell where the bullet hit.

'Not bad,' he said. 'You were a little to the left.'

He let her take a few more shots and then he took a few and didn't do much better. It didn't seem to bother him, though. She was ready for swearing or throwing the gun into the trees or worse, but he seemed like he was in a really good mood. It made her feel off-balance. Made her feel like there was a test she forgot to study for. Then he said they were done for now and they turned to go back inside and she understood. She could see Chase's face at the little bathroom window, could feel his Christmas present heavy in her hand.

&

Chase was supposed to be drawing triangles, he knew that. Everybody was leaning close over their pages. He looked out the window at the snowy field. The janitor was dumping garbage bags into the dumpster. Chase wished he was out there too, wearing work gloves and seeing his breath.

'Three right triangles and three scalene,' Miss Myers was saying.

He didn't know what a scalene was. Right was with the straight-up-and-down corners, so he drew three of those in a hurry as neatly as he could and then he sat looking up over the top of the blackboard. ABCDEFGHIJKLMNOPQRSTU VWXYZ. He looked around at the other kids. Scotty Matthews was wearing a sweater with snowmen on it and someone made fun of him at recess. His face got really red. Chase looked in his desk. His crayons were there. He went up to the front to sharpen his pencil. Miss Myers smiled at him and he smiled back. It was almost time for lunch.

'I'll want to see those triangles tomorrow,' Miss Myers said.

Haven would know how to do them.

&

He saw it. Like one dead eye filmed over. Like a tunnel that would kill you. Like a star coming to explode you.

He saw it. He saw it. Closer and closer.

It was morning. It was daylight. He shouldn't be thinking this. This was a nighttime thing. Stop. Stop. Stop thinking.

He felt it. Like black oil in his spine. Like night inside of him.
There.

He felt it.

over and over and over and over and over and over and over
and over and over and over

There.

Clickety clickety clickety clack.

His dad made him stand there on the tracks.

'Don't you move,' he said. 'Don't you dare move.'

Chicken.

'*Haven*, well, it's a place … where people rest.'

Her mother was explaining her name.

'Did anyone have it before me? Like my great-grandmother
or somebody?'

'No.'

Her mother was drinking coffee at the kitchen table. 'Nobody
in our family ever rested.'

Haven was working on a project for school. 'Do you have any
brothers or sisters?'

Her mother pulled her bathrobe together tighter. 'You used
to have an aunt,' she said.

Haven wrote down *Aunt*. 'Is she alive?'

'No, she's not, she's in Ireland.'

Haven wrote down *Ireland*.

'She didn't approve of your father.'

'Why not?'

Her mother looked at her across the table. 'You gonna write
this down?'

Haven put down her pencil. 'No.'

Her mother took a sip of her coffee. 'Well, she thought that your father wouldn't amount to much, I guess.' She took a graham cracker from the box. 'As if it had anything to do with her. So she married Francis whatsisfrigginname and shinnied herself over to Ireland. Guess that showed me.'

'Is she still there?'

Her mother shrugged. 'Don't know. Might be dead, for all I know about her now. I have to get dressed.'

She got up from the table and pulled at her robe again. Then she put the box of graham crackers on the counter, looked at her coffee mug and sighed and put it into the sink as if it were heavy.

'That's all I know,' she said, turning and walking towards the bedroom.

She wouldn't come out again for a while.

Haven. Where people rest, she wrote.

She finished the report by filling in her father's name and searching the bottom drawer in the kitchen for photographs. She found one of her school pictures that her dad had taken off the envelope from the school. Right where it said *Do Not Remove*.

'They expect you to do that, that's why they put the *Do Not Remove* there, they know you're gonna take it.'

He said he was going to put it into his wallet but it didn't look like he had. There was also a picture of Chase. She glued that onto the page and wrote *My Brother* under it in blue marker.

The morning the sweaty man in the suit came, Chase and Haven had been fighting about whether they would go swimming. They were both wearing their bathing suits. There was nothing clean to wear and it was really hot for still being June. Chase wanted to go but Haven was tired of sitting in the sun and sticking to a plastic chair by the pool or sinking slowly below the surface of the water and seeing how long she could stay under. When the man's car pulled into the driveway, they had been sitting on the trailer's steps for an hour not talking about it. There was barely enough room for the whole car because Chase's bike was lying next to the steps. The man got out and squinted at them in the sun.

'You guys live here?' the man asked. He had dark circles under his arms.

Haven nodded.

'Mom or Dad home?'

The man made Haven think of bread left in the bag on a hot day. Moist and soft.

Haven shook her head. She wasn't sure where Mom was and Dad was asleep on the floor at the end of the hall.

'Well … ' the man said.

He looked down the length of the outside of the trailer like he might see something of interest. Haven knew there was nothing but trailer for him to see. He reached into his pocket and pulled out a small white card and held it out for Haven to take.

'Your mom or dad get home you have them give me a call here.' He pointed to a number on the card. He took another look down the length of the trailer. 'I'll be waiting for a call,' he said.

He started to walk back to his car. 'Why aren't you two at school?' he turned and asked.

'My brother's sick,' Haven told him. 'He has bronchitis, and I have a field trip today but … I can't go … '

She knew he wouldn't ask why. She had an answer ready if he did.

He got back into his car and drove away.

'What's that about?' Chase asked Haven, trying to read the little card. There were blue letters on it that said *Children's Aid Society*.

'Nothing good,' Haven said, running her fingers over the little raised letters. The card was damp from the heat, from the man's hand and from being in his pocket. She knew nothing would happen. If the man was serious, he would have gone inside the trailer, not just looked at the outside of it. There was nothing to see on the outside. The outside never told you things. Chase picked at his knee. They never saw the man again.

Sometimes when his mother was cooking, Chase liked to sit at the kitchen table and do his homework. He liked the way the steam came from the pot when she made the noodles. Sometimes she made tuna casserole – Haven didn't like it but he did. The cheese was crispy on the top. Haven didn't like a lot of the food they had. 'Not hungry,' she'd say, pushing it away. Usually he got what Haven didn't eat. Sometimes his mother would have the radio on and she would sing along. If she was cooking she was happy and if she wasn't cooking she was sad. Sometimes she'd stay up cooking all night. Sometimes she didn't cook for days. She would lie in the bedroom with the blinds all the way down and a blanket hung over the window. They'd eat potato chips. They'd be quiet when they passed the door. Tiptoe.

Haven was around seven when the frogs died. It seemed like thousands of them at the time, a slow quilt of death across the lawn in front of the trailer, their white bellies up to the sky like the first snow.

'Wake up,' she told Chase, reaching over the warmth of his body and wiping more of the condensation from the window of the warming trailer.

'What? No,' he said. He never wanted to get out of bed or open his eyes.

'Yes,' she said, leaning on him and pressing her face against the wet glass. 'I think you should … '

'Why?'

'You just should, that's all,' she replied, sitting up and pulling a sweater over her head. 'Maybe they're not all dead … '

Outside the grass was cold and wet on her feet, the parts of the grass that were not covered with dead or dying frogs, and the smell in the air was like the smell after a rain when the worms come out of the ground, only more frog-like, and Haven pulled up the bottom of her nightie and gingerly stepped between the green legs and gaping mouths.

'What's going on?' Chase was out now and wiping his eyes.

'They're all dying,' Haven said, standing very still and turning around in a slow circle to survey the extent of the carnage.

'You're not going to cry, are you?' Chase said grumpily, sitting to pull on his rubber boots.

'No,' she said, 'I'm going to find out why.'

'Shit,' Chase said, the numbers of little bodies sinking in.

So she had tried to find out why, clumsily, in the trailer's tiny bathroom with the door closed and the sound of the TV in the next room – *Family Affair*, a show she would normally have been glued to with its promise of suddenly and inexplicably disappearing parents and a gruff but kindly uncle who took over everything and did a fine job of it. At the time she didn't think about why she loved the show so much, she just basked on the carpet in the warm glow of the coloured television that her mother said they couldn't afford and her father went out and bought one day and that they fought over every time somebody turned it on.

She left Chase watching it. She tried to find out why.

Spread before her on the floor of the bathroom was the body of a frog stretched coldly on its back, its arms and legs angled up, slightly stiff. She pushed down on them tentatively and they sprang back.

'Okay,' she whispered to the frog, 'okay.'

She reached into the pink zippered bag on the floor next to her and pulled out a small pair of scissors – cuticle scissors, her mother called them. Haven didn't know what *cuticle* meant and it bothered her.

'What does *cuticle* mean?' she had asked her mother.

'What does it matter?' had been the answer.

She thought it best to start between the legs and cut up towards the throat. She was a bit uneasy at first, but as soon as she poked through the rubbery skin and made the first cut she was okay.

'I gotta go.' Chase was knocking at the door and pulling on the knob.

'Not now,' Haven said, snipping through the tissue and watching it spring away from the silver metal as she cut.

'Yes, now,' Chase pleaded. 'I gotta go.'

She sighed and carefully laid the scissors to one side on the furry pink bath mat and stood up to let him in.

'Don't let the cat in here,' she said as he squeezed past.

He stopped and stared at the open frog.

'You're gonna be in so much trouble,' he said.

'I'm not,' Haven told him forcefully, 'because you're not going to tell.'

Chase continued to stare, his mouth open.

'Okay, I'm not,' he said with his eyes still on the frog. 'But I get to watch.'

'Okay.'

She could feel Chase breathing next to her as she picked up the scissors and carefully started again, finishing the long cut to the throat.

'What's inside it?' Chase asked.

'Quiet,' Haven told him and then laughed because she realized that quiet was exactly what was inside a frog.

She wasn't sure what to do next. She continued the cut up the centre of the throat, but she cut too deeply and a lot of blood started to leak out.

'Gross,' Chase said with barely contained excitement.

'Pass me some toilet paper,' Haven told him and she mopped carefully at the spill.

She sat looking at her work and thinking.

'Well?' Chase was becoming impatient with the pace of the show.

Haven backtracked and began to very slowly slice across the top of the frog's chest down from her first cut to just under each arm.

'You just have to be very careful,' she told Chase.

'Or what?' he asked.

'You just do, that's all,' she said.

'He's already dead, you know,' Chase said. 'You can't kill him.'

Haven thought about what would happen if their mother or father came in, which was more and more likely the longer they were both in here.

'You should go back,' she said.

'I'll tell,' Chase threatened.

'Fine.'

She picked up the scissors again and finished two cuts from her first cut down to the legs. 'Now we peel it open,' she told him.

'Like a banana,' Chase said.

'I suppose,' she said, shaking her head as if dealing with someone half her age.

She gingerly pulled at the flaps of skin and coaxed them along with the help of the scissors. She was surprised how easily everything came apart.

'There,' she said.

'What's that?' Chase asked, pointing to a large lump at the centre of the frog.

Haven peered closer. 'Its heart,' she decided. 'Or its lungs … maybe its lungs.'

'Oh.'

'Its lungs,' she decided. 'Where it breathes.'

'Not anymore.'

'No. Where it breathed then.'

Haven sat back again and wiped her hair away from her face with her arm.

'What are you two doing in there?'

Her mother's voice had the sound in it that pulled coldly at the bottom of Haven's belly.

'Nothing,' she said, quickly picking up the small corpse.

'Pooing,' Chase added, lifting the lid of the toilet.

Haven dropped the frog in.

'Done,' Chase called as Haven flushed. They stood and watched the little body twirl in smaller and smaller circles and they held their breath as it caught briefly at the bottom and then gave up and was carried off to wherever things flushed down the toilet went. Away.

'Hurry up.'

'Yes,' Haven said quickly. *Yes* was the best word to say when her mother's voice sounded like that. She elbowed Chase in the ribs.

'Yes,' he echoed.

Yes.

&

Ivy leaned over him and breathed onto the frost on the window behind the bed. Her little white T-shirt pulled up. Wiped the cold glass with her wrist. Smiled down.

Gone.

&

One morning Chase called to Haven from their room. He was bored reading the same comics. He was sitting on their mattress with her bear on his lap.

'Look what I found,' he said.

The morning sun shone through the yellow sheet covering the window. Chase was pulling slowly at something in the bear's belly.

'Don't,' Haven said, putting down her bowl of bread and milk and reaching for the bear. When there was no cereal they tore up pieces of bread and floated them in milk. When there was bread.

'Is there cereal?' Chase eyed the bowl and held the bear up for her to see.

'No. What?' she asked, looking at the bear's belly where Chase had torn a hole and the fluffy white stuffing was coming out.

'Here,' he said, taking it back and poking his fingers into the hole. She had never given the bear a name. It was just the bear. Sometimes she slept with it, sometimes she didn't.

Chase pulled his fingers back out and he was holding a small green plastic snake.

'As if,' she said, eyeing it as he held it in front of her face.

'I swear to God,' he said.

She hadn't believed him, and she had given him a whack in the head for making a hole in her bear, but he didn't cry because they never let their parents see them fight and he swore even when they were grown up that he had really found the snake inside the bear.

&

Once his father played army men with him. They used the couch pillows on the floor and made forts with slippers and boots. Felt like warm syrup dripping down.

&

'Do you have a plan?'

'I've never had a plan.'

'But do you know what you'd do?'

'I wouldn't do anything,' he said. He knew it was a lie. She wasn't sure.

'Chase?'

'Forget it.'

&

Haven remembered being very small and lying on the bathroom floor with her head tucked up between the toilet and the shower stall listening to the roar of the water rumbling through the tin wall. Waiting for it to be warm. Her head rested on the pink fringed carpet that wrapped around the base of the toilet. The hanging toilet paper fluttered over her and above that was the little window that wound open and shut with a crank. You could stand on the toilet and crank that window as far as it would go and you could see out to the lean-to shed and the trees. Smell the fresh air and the metal of the screen. She remembered the pink plastic shower curtain stained like coffee at the bottom. She remembered her mother's hands on her back and in her hair and then squinting up her eyes against the shampoo water. Her mother singing something. Being under the shower water holding her breath as long as she could so she didn't get a mouthful of soap and the muffled sounds of everything. The suds winding down and away. Her mother's voice above her sounding like it was wrapped in towels: 'Haven ... Haven ... Time to get out.'

Her mother wrapping her then in a towel. The water swirling around the drain. Her hair stuck to her forehead. The cool air from the little window.

She didn't know if it was one time or all the times rolled together.

In pre-med they played a tape of what it sounded like for the baby inside the mother's womb. It was the same sound. The sound of rushing water. The instructor turned it up loud. Haven had to leave the room.

Couldn't breathe.

&

Her mother was talking again and it wasn't to anyone who was there. It wasn't to anyone that Haven knew.

'Yes, yes, yes,' she said

and

'I will ... I will ... '

like it was someone she was afraid of.

'I know.'

She was staring straight out the window at the snow. Her small hands were white on the counter. Haven studied her toast. Her father got up and walked out.

'Mom?'

'I will ... yes ... '

Chase would be up soon.

'Mom?'

When she was little, Haven had this house in her head that had nothing to do with the trailer that they lived in, nothing to do with the life that they led. It was defined by the things that it was not. It was not next to a driving range. Golf balls did not hit the roof. It did not have a porch that could fall on you and kill you. There wasn't a big crack in the window that was taped over with newspaper. The screens weren't all busted. There wasn't a lone boot just lying out on the front lawn. It was not dark at all hours with the curtains closed.

It was someplace you didn't have to have your pillow over your head so that you couldn't hear. The house in her head was quiet and filled with light. It was a place you could walk around in without always being careful. Without the feeling that you were being hunted. It was a place you wanted to go into, not get out of. The house in her head was the place that she went when there was nowhere else for her to go.

&

Chase was in a ball on the bed reading *Jughead's Double Digest*. The one with Jughead and Big Ethel on the cover kissing. Jughead was looking at a hamburger through the window of Pop's Chock-lit Shoppe. Chase was reading 'Somebody Snitched.' He'd read it before. He kept reading the same page over and over.

'Oh, poor Juggie!' Betty was crying.

'What about poor Jug?' Archie in the yellow checked shirt he always wore.

'Some fink ratted on our good friend!' It was good to have friends.

'I thought I was the only one who knew he did it!' Archie was confused.

'You knew too?'

'But I didn't tell anyone!'

Chase looked at the bruise on his arm. It hurt when he touched it just a little. It was raised up like it was angry. It would go away. It was like a bee sting. He had to not touch it and it would go away. He'd wear his long sleeves tomorrow. It wouldn't be too hot.

'Only you can prevent forest fires.' Smokey the Bear was talking to a couple of kids with matches.

His long-sleeved shirt scratched at the back of his neck on hot days.

Big Moose was going to clobber Jughead because he thought Jughead had kissed his girlfriend. He didn't, though. Somehow he'd get away.

School was easy. Sometimes it was somebody's birthday and they would bring in cupcakes from home. They'd all sing 'Happy Birthday' and then the chocolate icing or vanilla. He liked the vanilla. He was undiagnosed, he heard Miss Myers say to another teacher once when he came back in at recess to get his jacket. They both looked up at him and stopped talking. Chase told everyone his birthday was in July.

The big field trip at the end of the year in Grade 3 was to the Science and Technology Museum in Ottawa. It was almost an hour from Kemptville to the east end of Ottawa by bus and Chase had never been there. You had to bring in a dollar to go, and Chase had started collecting the money weeks before the trip. Haven helped him in the morning, making sure his money was in his lunch bag and signing his permission slip. Careful with the curving lines.

Chase had almost thrown up on the bus with the excitement and with the length of the trip, which was longer than any he had taken before. It took over an hour for the bus to get to the museum and Chase clutched his lunch and peered through the grimy window at a lighthouse that was just sitting in the front yard. Cars drove by like there was nothing unusual about a lighthouse in a front yard. Chase had never been to the city before. Maybe it wasn't unusual.

Everyone milled about in the lobby while the teachers went and talked to a lady behind glass about tickets. Some of the kids started to go ahead into the displays but Chase stayed where he'd been told. He didn't know how he'd ever get home if he got lost – there was a flat tire on the car and his father hadn't fixed it yet. There was a little movie theatre and there were some little towers with glass boxes on them and inside the glass boxes there were some Indian arrowheads and some pictures of people from the olden days.

Chase stood anxiously to one side watching.

One of the mothers came over and read names from a slip of paper. 'Chase, Dylan, Teresa, Sean and Lisa ... you're all with me.'

They sorted themselves out and began to make their way down the hallway past round Styrofoam depictions of the solar system.

Mrs. Daniels, who was in the lead, told them that first they would see the crooked kitchen. Chase had heard about the crooked kitchen at school. It was a real kitchen that was tilted up at one end and it was supposed to make you sick when you walked in it.

'My brother puked up his whole breakfast,' Alicia Walters had informed a circle at recess that Chase had been on the fringes of.

'They had to shut the whole place down for two hours while they cleaned it all up. It was a big breakfast.'

Chase didn't care about any of that. There was a little wooden staircase that led up to the door of the kitchen and Mrs. Daniels' group was perched and waiting.

'My sister told me this was really cool,' Anika Stewart told Chase.

Anika Stewart had never spoken to Chase before unless it was to tell him to take two steps back and stop being weird.

'I know,' Chase said. He didn't know what else to say so he looked away and held his lunch bag a little tighter.

This is like the end of the world, he thought as he stepped into the room behind Anika.

He didn't know why he thought that but suddenly it was true. There was something about the little room and the way the other kids slid and angled through it that held him and would not let him go. There were black iron railings that were supposed to keep everyone safe that Chase somehow missed and slid under, ending up somewhere near the stove. By the time he was pulled out he was a little shaken.

'Come along, dear,' Mrs. Daniels said, guiding him out of the room. 'We'll get you sorted out.'

Chase thought maybe he would throw up but in the end he didn't. The other kids came out dizzy and laughing and talking about the kitchen and Chase was quiet, hoping nobody would talk about him getting stuck by the stove.

They saw a display about the history of planes and there were windows you could look into and see little people in scenes with planes. You could push a red button and lights in the scenes would come on.

There was one scene with two men in a snowstorm and they were waiting for a plane to find them. When you pressed the button their lantern came on and a little light on the plane flying overhead. Chase thought they had done a really good job making it all seem real. He wanted to stay there looking at it and pressing the button all day. Guiding the plane through the storm and saving the men. They looked pretty cold.

'Come along now,' Mrs. Daniels said. 'We have to meet the other groups at the trains in five minutes.'

Chase thought he was going to throw up. Why was Mrs. Daniels talking about trains? How could there be trains in a museum? They were inside a building. You can't have big things like trains inside a building. His teacher hadn't said anything about trains when she was explaining the trip at the blackboard. Chase wouldn't have come. He would have stayed home. He was thinking all this as they struggled to keep up with Mrs. Daniels, whose heels clicked with authority on the hard floor as she weaved through the crowds. He looked all over for a way out. He didn't want to get left behind and lost but he didn't want to keep going. Something bad would happen. Then the smell hit him. The dusty coal smell from the wood they used to make the railway tracks. Mrs. Daniels turned a corner and Chase saw a break in the wall of people and there they were lined up in an enormous room, at least eight train engines, like black mountains.

Chase froze.

It was like a scene from a movie he had seen once on that *Wonderful World of Disney* where Mickey Mouse had these brooms that came to life and started carrying these buckets of water around. It was like all the trains turned towards him as soon as he got to the huge door, like they could smell that it was him and that he was afraid of them, like kids said that dogs could tell if you're afraid of them by the smell you give off.

Chase fell to his knees.

Around him there was a hum and a buzzing like all of the people had started yelling at the same time, and he felt his hands and feet go cold. He could see the legs of people brushing past him but he could not see Mrs. Daniels' clicking shoes or the shoes of the other kids. They had all just gone right into the train room like it was nothing. The huge blank headlights of the trains turned and stared at him and the burnt smell of the wood stuck in his nose and throat. He had trouble getting his breath and he was aware that his voice was somewhere in the buzzing sound and that he was moaning softly. He couldn't feel his tongue.

Chase peed.

He wasn't really aware that he had gone to the bathroom, just that his legs were wet and that there was a puddle around his knees. The trains just kept getting bigger and closer even though he wasn't moving. He felt the air pushing into him like little pins and the world going up and around him like a funnel. Like he was on the track and the train was coming out of the tunnel.

'Hey there,' a voice said.

There was a big man leaning over him with his hands on Chase's shoulders but Chase couldn't see his face. He was at the end of the tunnel. He was in the dark.

'Hey, what's up?' the man said.

Chase tried to work his mouth.

'I think there's something wrong,' Chase said.

looks like a flame with its leaves coming out ... in colours like a tree, like the wind when it blows a tree in the fall with the colours like a flame falling like someone singing opera music like on the radio with the little light-up marker that shows the station like a candle like a little fire like it would be beside a canal in the dark like there were people around it cooking something yeah a ring of softer light around it in the dark like it would come up like a light to the stars and the smell of the smoke from way up high and next to a lake in the night at the edge its edges worn down by the water and the ice worn away like something softer scraping in the night over the years rubbing down the smooth surface of the water smooth surface of the rock like the grey land all around like the snow like the snow melting from a flame around it all stretched out over the water of the lake yeah or like one of those holes you make to fish in the ice you see it from way down like a fish would like a little circle of the sky like a door like the lights at night like a city like Christmas lights the way lights twinkle like they're stars like that like the little ball of light when you turn off the TV and where does it go into the dark like all light eventually goes into the dark like that

    into the dark
    music in his head

    Lengths of bones can help establish race
    Pelvic bones determine sex
    Scapula very deep, through-and-through cut
      mark – lines up with cut mark on rib
    Stabbing wound to back
    Hole on back, difficult to determine cause due
      to near mummification of body
    Unlikely to have been gunshot
    Possible further deterioration due to insects

Haven wiped the big magnifying lens. Continued writing. Then she shoved the notes aside and sat thinking of scars. She was very tired of university already. Very few people sat on a sunny spring morning and thought about scars, she thought. Very few professions demanded it. She ran her fingers along the raised ridge of too-white skin that ran along her calf: twenty-three ghostly railway ties stretching from here … to there. Here … to there. Thought about the way the touch of her fingertips felt like an echo, the way in which her body recorded the events of her own history. This was deciding, she thought, this was making a decision to make her history – to make anyone's history – count. Ken had never touched her scar. It was important to love what you do.

&

Not that he thought things would be better, just different. They were for a while. He was still in a basement. Living in North York wasn't that much different than living in Kemptville. The food was better.

He worked at 7-Eleven where he looked after the hot-dog roller, stocked the shelves, rotated the milk, replaced the Slurpee cups. It was all the way downtown, so he took a bus to the subway and the subway to work. He had a pass.

He thought Toronto would make things different. It did, in a way. He missed Haven but otherwise it was okay. He called her on the phone at night when it was cheaper. Sometimes he worked the midnight shift and sometimes he worked days. It wasn't bad. It was okay. Then Ivy came in to buy an iced tea. She took off her bike helmet at the cash.

'How much is that?' she asked.

Chase had never wanted so much to say something good.

'Seventy-nine cents,' was all he could come up with.

'Are you sure?'

It wasn't. It was eighty-nine cents.

'We're having a special,' he said.

'Really?' And she smiled at him.

She counted out the change on the counter. There was a lady behind her with a *Toronto Sun* and some Breathsavers.

'Kind of,' he said.

'Thanks,' she said, taking a straw.

'You bet.'

He thought about her until she came back the next day. Then he thought about her more.

'Any specials today?' she'd ask.

'Straws are free.'

'Aren't they usually free?'

'Not the bendy ones.' He slid them out from behind the lotto machine. 'We charge two cents for those.'

Ivy's mouth curled at the corner. 'But not today?' she asked.

'That's right.'

He could see them married one day. Bike girl. Counter boy. They could have children and train them to work in the service industry. They could have children, and they could treat them well.

'What's free today?' she asked the next morning.

'Burritos.'

'They are not.'

'They are if you let me take you over there and buy you one,' he said, pointing across the street at the Mexican restaurant. He'd been planning how to say that for three days. She said okay.

&

The lean-to was where their father kept the lawnmower in the winter, under the plywood, wrapped in a large sheet of plastic. Once Chase had helped him clean the blades of all the caked dead grass at the end of the summer before the mower got put away.

'You don't take the time to take it off now it'll just be all one piece in the spring, grass and metal and all.' He pressed his lips hard together and took another run at the green felt of the grass with a butter knife. They had a screwdriver and a butter knife and they worked away at peeling the grass off like wallpaper. Chase bit his lips together like his dad did. He knew his mother would be pissed about the butter knife. He kept his mouth shut about that.

'Shit!' His dad's hand had slipped and driven hard down into the well of the mower. He pulled it out bleeding.

'Shit,' he said again, looking at his hand.

He glanced at Chase. 'Sorry,' he said, 'sorry.'

He lit a cigarette with a shaking hand. And they went back to work on the blades.

&

They found the cigarette in the lean-to. Little kids with a treasure. There were cigarettes all over the house, but somehow finding one outside in the winter made it theirs to do with what they wanted. Years later, Haven would remember the two of them kneeling there in their snow pants like grim pilgrims.

'What should we do with it?' Chase cradled it in a mittened hand.

'Let me think.'

She remembered that Chase wanted to try smoking it but she decided that they should destroy it. In the end they had each taken turns mashing it into the ground with their boots, then dropping rocks on it, the brown-grey circle slowly becoming wider and wider in the snow.

These thoughts in his head. Riding his bike. Heaven is nice. Leading you, yeah heaven is nice, when you go to it. It's okay. The snow is in April, showers in May. Smells nice when you take a sniff. Over there. The smell of under the leaves still wet from the winter. When I get that radio it'll be good and all I know is next day or this. Always the next day. We'll see, though. Maybe I'll get the radio. Maybe not. Probably not. Always the next day there's calmness. There's nothing. Always bad and then quiet the next day. There through the trees. Sticks. On you. You can never be sure when you're having fun. I hear you I hear you all the time. Always think of a pool like swimming, just think of a pool. Peaceful there. I hear you and I worry to go that way. From time to time and I yeah … follow a thing right to the end the colours through those trees like a mirror a squirrel see it's a long world well I tell you a long world … that's what they say the one thing is that when he's like that he's like that when he's, but other times too if they're even home the home of the brave the home of the brave maybe not

I hear you I hear you all the time.

Heaven is nice. Beautiful. The home of the brave.

The bear was the most real thing Chase had ever seen. First it was a shape in his mind. It was a shifting in the trees and a sound. Then it was real. It was the realest thing ever.

'I could kill the both of you right here and now,' Mary told them after she'd found them once with a pack of matches.

But she wouldn't really do that and they knew it. And that was the difference.

&

Chase learned how to play at school. You thought up the word and then you counted the letters and then you drew in the man while somebody guessed. Haven didn't want to play. She had math homework to do. It was Saturday morning and she wanted to do math homework instead of playing hangman.

He sat at the kitchen table and set up the word blanks and the noose. He tried to do a good job on the wood thing that holds up the noose. He tried to do the best job he could because there was no one to play with anyway. He made the wood grain with the knots in it and he drew little blades of grass and a flower. His tongue pressed between his lips. He thought the flower was a nice touch.

He took the paper and pencil over to the couch and showed it to his father. His father was watching *The Galloping Gourmet* on TV.

'S'good … who're you hangin'?' his father asked.

'Nobody,' Chase said.

The Galloping Gourmet was slicing up onions and pretending to cry. You could tell he was pretending. The audience was laughing.

'All this bugger has to do is cook a meal a day,' his father said, pointing his beer at the screen, 'and drink a boatload of red wine.'

'Do you want to have a game?' Chase asked.

'What?'

'It's a game called hangman I could show you.'

His father kept watching the screen. The Galloping Gourmet was sliding the sliced onions into a pan.

Chase stood waiting.

'Sure,' his father said.

It took a long time for his father to get the word. Chase ran out of body parts to draw so he added other things to the drawing instead: more flowers, a bird, a rocket up in the sky. He wasn't sure if it was because his father was watching TV – the Galloping Gourmet was bringing someone down from the audience to sit with him on the stage and eat the food he had made – or if he was just pretending not to know the word.

The word was *Jello*.

His father got down to the last letter and tried *hello*.

'Nope.'

Yellow.

'There's no W.'

Mellow?

'Dad, there's no W.'

'Oh.' His father opened another beer. '*Fellow?*'

'Dad … '

'What?'

Finally he got *Jello* and then they watched the *Pink Panther* cartoon show and Chase kept drawing other little things around the hanged man. An airplane. The sun. His father opened another beer. Chase didn't ask if he wanted to play again.

He just wanted to see the noodle box. The Hamburger Helper. See if it was yellow cheese or orange and what shape noodles it was.

He was going to see the box when he got pushed into the metal edge of the table. Little metal edge on the table that left stripes in the bruise later. He felt the rattling chair on top of him as his father threw it out of his way.

'Told you ta keep outta my way. You're always everywhere, the two of you – under my feet.'

Haven helped him get up. He was crying. Stared at him. Helped him to stop. Her eyes telling him no.

They went in the bedroom and he put his face in the pillow.

'Turn over.'

They looked at the bruise, red like a rash. She pulled his sweater down.

'I've seen worse,' she decided.

'I just wanted to see the box,' Chase told her, controlling his voice.

'You have to be more careful, that's all,' she said.

'Okay.'

One morning a couple of days later he was out with his dad who had said it was time for a walk. They were out looking for bottles and cans they could get refund money for. Haven wasn't allowed to come. He knew she was watching him out the door.

'Look down there,' his dad said, pointing his stick into the ditch at something red under the long dry grass.

Chase scrambled down into the ditch. The red was next to the pipe thing that carried the water through and Chase stopped to look in. It was cool and dark out of the sun and every little sound he made was echoed. He heard a car crunch and stop on the gravel above and his father's voice and the voice of another man. He picked the red out of the grass and found a Canadian bottle. His dad would like that. He would say, 'Good, put it in the bag.'

Chase climbed back up and his dad was talking to Ed, who was leaning out the window of his pickup.

'Well, what's new, big man?' Ed asked Chase when he saw him appear out of the ditch.

Chase smiled and pulled up his shirt to show the bruise now spread and purple across his side.

'This.'

Then his father's eyes on him.

'Hey, that's a good one, how'd you get that?' Ed was asking.

Chase put his shirt down.

'He fell,' his father said.

Cold.

&

You saw more polka dots on Aunt Mary than you did on most people, he thought. Usually green ones. He assumed it was because she'd lived in Ireland for a while and that's just the way people dressed there. It was partly that and it was partly that Aunt Mary was not a small woman and thought that polka dots lessened the situation – which they did not. Such matters were lost on Chase, who thought of his aunt not as a set of dimensions but more as a force of nature, like a glacier or the orbit of the earth.

He showed her a picture he had painted of Haven.

'You're a painter?' Mary asked. 'Next you'll be slicin' off bits of yourself and leavin' them around the house for the rest of us to find.'

'I like painting,' he said.

'Do you think it'd be a burden to like doing something that was in any way useful to the rest of the world or could bring a dollar into this house?'

Which, he thought at the age of thirty-five, perhaps he had never done.

'Her hair's green,' she said.

'I like green.'

'People don't have green hair,' she decided.

He showed it to Haven.

'My hair's not green,' Haven said critically. 'It's black.'

'It's green in this painting,' he told her.

'I can see that.'

But she didn't mind. 'I like it,' she said.

So he had painted seventeen more, most of them with hair the colour of Mary's polka dots.

'They've invented these things,' his aunt told him one morning, moving aside one of the paintings to reach for the jam, 'called cameras. Apparently some find them quite useful, and you can print the pictures any size you want. Which makes it easier to find the damned milk ... '

'It's in the fridge,' Chase had told her.

She gave him the look.

&

Haven remembered being little and playing on the kitchen floor. She had some dolls or some cars and she'd be playing at her mother's feet as she stood at the sink. She'd march the dolls back and forth or drive the cars around the corner of the cupboards, but really the whole game was about getting closer to her mother without being seen. Or it was about being seen, she thought, really it was about that.

&

Shit.

was the first thing her father would say each morning. Sometimes he'd say *shit* and then cough. Sometimes he'd cough and then say *shit*. Sometimes he wouldn't cough. But he always said *shit* and she could hear it, and everything else, through the panelled walls.

One time in winter Chase had been sick and her mother had been in bed for a few days so it was just her and her dad having cornflakes. She was careful not to take too much milk.

'We should do something, eh? Just the two of us,' her dad said suddenly.

'What?' she asked.

'I don't know. Go somewhere, leave the sick ones here. We could drive down to Niagara Falls – I've never been there.'

She was excited and scared at the same time. He wouldn't really do it.

'We could go over the Falls in a barrel.'

Now she knew he wouldn't do it. She poured a little more milk.

'Not too much,' he said.

They watched *Sesame Street* on the couch.

'Shit. This family never goes anywhere,' he said.

He picked up the sports section from the floor. Haven went to check on Chase.

'What are you doing?' Chase asked from the bed.

'Nothing,' she told him.

&

One morning shortly after Haven returned from the hospital, she woke up just before dawn, crawled over Chase's sleeping body and wandered into the kitchen. She had no slippers or pyjamas, just a bathrobe and underwear that said *Tuesday*. Her feet were cold and sticky on the floor. The counter light was on and next to the coffee maker was the can of ground coffee and a spoon, loose coffee spread across the white counter in a wide arc and a box of filters on the floor. She cleaned it up and looked out the window at the lawn and trees emerging slowly from the darkness. Saw herself, painted on the night and centred in the mirrored yellow rectangle of electric light. Looking down. She put the coffee away and wandered into the living room, where she had found her father sitting on the couch, just sitting there and crying quietly. Without thinking about it, she wrapped her robe again and curled up next to him, taking his arm and placing it around her shoulders, and they stayed there like that until the rest of the house began to rise and stir. They never talked about it after that and she was pretty sure that he didn't remember it.

&

She didn't care.

She didn't care.

She knew there was some smell from her parents, from home, that always stuck to them. The sickening sweet smell of the Coke that the vodka went into and the beer, and the stale cigarette smell. She couldn't tell which one she carried with her or if it was both but she knew that something followed her, that something in the schoolyard set her apart. Set them apart. Standing with Chase before the bell rang, holding their books. Alone.

&

He could be washing dishes when it came to him, driving to the Mac's for cigarettes or milk, or just sitting – often it was just sitting. The train and its dark threatening metal, its plaintive whistle warning and its one slowly increasing eye. His father cracking the sunflower seeds, one by one, spitting their shells onto the dry ground.

'Stand, stand ... Don't you move ... ' His father's voice a rasping cigarette hatchet.

His father had no face then. A voice, a pair of hands, a smell.

Chase drove the Jeep back to the spot from time to time – it was almost an hour away from where he lived now. Couldn't afford it but he'd bought the Jeep anyway. Fifteen hundred for an old YJ.

As is. Down the curving gravel road with the climbing walls of trees on either side – poplars and birches, evergreens – till he reached the place where the road snaked into an S curve, lifting over a level crossing at the centre of a clearing. Crunching gravel under his shoes and the tanging smell of the old tar. He was afraid to go back at night – just in the morning with the damp still on the tar-soaked wood. There was never anyone there. The track continued over the crossing but also ended in two branches that he thought were called sidings. Three derelict box cars stood on the tracks, gradually evaporating into their surroundings, and one smaller car caked with rust that looked like some sort of maintenance car.

If you stood on the track and peered into the distance, it seemed to go on forever, like a textbook example of a vanishing point. He'd left the keys in the Jeep on, the soft notes of the warning chimes echoing through the open window. He squinted into the dawn, unsure if trains still ran here.

'Don't you move,' his father's voice threatening. 'Don't you tell anybody about this … '

And the train coming. Coming now. Rumble.

This can't be good for anyone's soul, Haven thought. She'd learned about the soul at school. She imagined her soul like a sheet of paper. Clean white paper sandwiched inside her chest between her organs and everything that she did would pass through it like the filter on a cigarette. It would get dark over time. The bad stuff would be absorbed for you but eventually if there was too much of it your soul would get too clogged up, like a furnace filter with dead bugs and hair. It wouldn't be good anymore – it wouldn't be able to protect you. She pictured the movie in Science about semi-permeable membranes. Little silver bubbles in black and white. Rising. Or a soul was like water, always finding its own level. Sometimes her mother straightened her coat for her before she went out to the bus. Sometimes she made lunches for her and for Chase and she gave them to Haven on her way out the door.

'Take your brother's,' she'd say.

It had been a long time.

&

'I don't want ham sandwiches in my lunch anymore,' Haven announced to Aunt Mary after they moved.

Mary paused over the white beds of sliced bread. 'Make your own then.'

Haven toyed with her cereal for a moment. 'I used to do that,' she said.

Mary waited.

'I know you did,' Mary said quietly, eyeing Haven over the shelter of the cereal box.

'Me and Chase, I made lunches for both of us.'

'I know that too.'

'I could do it again,' she said.

Eyes locked.

'Do it then.'

The plastic clock above the stove clicked.

And then.

'Ham's okay.'

Mary forced them to love her. It was against their instinct.

'C'mere, they're ready. And take your brother's.'

Handed her the bags. Touched her on the shoulder. Then on the arm.

'There,' she said.

Walking out into the snow.

There.

&

There are no prizes. Nothing but Crackerjack and box. All of her money, what little she had after paying student loans and every-thing else – April's dance lessons – went to keeping Mary in this place. It wasn't a bad place. It was quite good, actually. It was what Mary needed. Haven had to keep working. Chase couldn't do it. Chase wished he could do it. Wanted to do it. But Chase could-n't do it and that was all.

She did her best when she visited. Sometimes she made mis-takes. There had been nothing about Alzheimer's in pre-med. It had been all about cutting bodies open, not about what to do when something had come in the night and emptied out all of the memories. When somehow a tube had been hooked into the side of the head to slowly drain out everything that Mary remem-bered, everything she knew in the world. It had all gone so fast. It seemed like days ago that she was standing in the kitchen telling Mary she was leaving med school and going back to school to be a teacher. Two years. Gone.

Haven set her Tim's cup down on the window sill.

'Are you feeling too warm?' she asked.

It was June and they had Mary in a February sweater. Haven pulled at her own top.

'Is this too warm, are you hot?'

Mary looked at her. Nodded.

Advanced Alzheimer's.

Just about everything drained right out. But now and then a smile. Now and then a touch.

Haven reached for the bottom of the sweater and started to pull it over Mary's head and suddenly Mary was screaming as if she were on fire.

'What? What? What is it?' Haven cried, frantically pulling at the sweater but Mary's arms were caught up in it and thrashing and she kept on screaming.

A nurse ran in and took over. That was how Haven would remember it. The nurse took the situation away from Haven like you would calmly take something dangerous away from a small child.

'Here,' she said to Haven, firmly setting her to one side towards the window and then saying, 'Mary ... Mary,' and then gently pulling the sweater up and over her head. Mary immediately stopped screaming and her gaze settled on the window and then on a car entering the parking lot.

'She's got no sense of time now,' the nurse said, looking to Haven and folding the sweater, 'so she has no way of knowing how long she's been inside that sweater when you pull it over her like that.'

The nurse tried to smile. Haven was aware that her hand was at her own mouth and she could picture it there, the way it would look, like she was in shock, but she couldn't move it away. Like some woman in a movie standing in a corner with her hand over her mouth. Like she'd seen a ghost.

The nurse placed the sweater on the nightstand next to the bed.

'You didn't know that,' the nurse told her. 'And there's no harm done. Look ... ' She pointed to Mary, who was now looking up at the two of them as if nothing had happened.

The nurse took a plastic cup with a straw and placed the straw at Mary's mouth.

'This is cool water, Mary,' she said. 'You drink some of this cool water, it's nice.'

Haven recognized the nurse's voice. It was the same voice she used herself with the high-needs students in her class now that she was teaching. This was the voice she would now be using with her aunt. With Mary. Haven willed her hand to move away from her mouth.

She had no idea how long she'd had her head inside the sweater. There was no way Haven could have known that it had gotten this bad. She was doing the best she could. It wasn't this bad last week. How bad would it be a week from now?

'Thank you,' she said to the nurse.

'Mm-hm,' the nurse answered. In the same voice she had used with Mary.

Here's the thing, Chase thought, the people and the way that they moved. The way they moved. Like they all had somewhere to go. And then somewhere to go back to when they were done. He drank the rest of his Golden from the coffee mug and kept peering out at Prescott Street. Grimy window. Years gone by. Because he had worked here for a while, they served him before noon. As long as he had it in a coffee mug so no one could tell. As long as he ordered some food to go with it. And they never made him pay full price.

The clock ticking. Children working in their books. Seven minutes to the recess bell. She never counted the clock. Laughed to herself at teachers who did. Six minutes.

Chase saw the comic book for the second day in a row. Second day of life in Grade 4. The first day was a Tuesday and then it was a Wednesday and the comic book was still staring out at him from the back corner where they hung up their coats. Usually Chase was in a hurry to get to his desk and check on his pencils and make sure everything was ready and then listen to Miss Myers tell them what they would be doing and anything that was new. He didn't like it when there were new things. Sometimes she would have an announcement from the office or she'd have something to tell them about her life outside of school. Once she told them about going to a mall and buying shoes and Chase imagined her shining new shoes clicking down the smooth floor of the shopping centre. Clip clip clip clip. She had lines up the backs of her legs. Those were stockings. They wrapped tight around her legs. Little lines like a net when she sat to read them a story and they went around and around her legs like a circle and they went around and around and up. Sometimes when they sat to listen to a story, kids would reach up and touch her legs because they were so smooth. Chase just listened.

It was a Donald Duck comic. *Donald Duck and Friends*. His friends were Huey, Dewey and Louie, his Uncle Scrooge, and Daisy, and then there'd be Mickey Mouse or Pluto or Goofy or that Professor guy. Those were the ones that were in the other stories. The cover was red and blue and yellow and green and it was shining like the new pastels in the box when you were the first to use them before everyone else got them and smudged them all up with different colours and turned them to mud. They were pure. They were something that was new but always the same. Each story in the comic was a new one he had never read and they were all pressed tight tight together now and if he took the comic home he could read each one of them by peeling them apart one at a time. They were waiting. The pages smelled like grass. You could feel the ink. Take it take it take it take it take it take it take it take it take it he took it and walked quickly to his desk.

It was wrong, though, and he spent the next three weeks ripping it up bit by bit and flushing it down the toilet when he went to the bathroom. Watching the bright colours float around and around round round round and down. It was wrong to take things and that was the only way to make it better. You could fix things. You could.

&

His father told them that the cat got hit by a school bus. They didn't believe him because he had never liked that cat.

And it was July.

&

Haven listened to her first-year anatomy lecturer talk about forensics and autopsies. Plaque-clogged arteries in the abdomen meant a red-meat lover, black-encrusted lungs meant an addiction to nicotine. Each body carried secrets. A faint indentation in the ulna was evidence of an arm broken in childhood. Each body carried secrets.

The first time Haven and her lab partners gathered around the corpse they decided to call him Fred. Giving the thing a name seemed to make it easier to take it apart. Without a name it was just too cold. Ian began their first incision.

'How will we know if we're going too deep?' Ian asked the group.

'He'll scream,' Ken muttered.

They all laughed. Nervous.

&

Haven was used to it now. She was used to it. She returned to table 17 with a hacksaw and a set of shears. With the rest of the group watching, she began to sever the ribs with the shears, the first step in freeing the breastplate from its protective position over the lungs and heart. The sound of the metal crunching through the soft bone and marrow slowed her down a little. Then she kept going.

In each lab there was a sign. DO NOT PUT HUMAN TISSUE IN GARBAGE CANS.

She remembered what her lab instructor had told the group on the day of the first incision. Following instructions, Haven had slowly sliced halfway down the sternum with the scalpel, tracing a path from the nape of Fred's neck. Then she had made a careful vertical incision halfway across the left side of Fred's chest. Then she had peeled back the skin. Like peeling an orange.

Carefully she scraped away the top layer of fatty tissue below the superficial fascia. The words and the actions. Say the words in your head while you do the actions. *Superficial fascia. The lateral thoracic vein.* The inside of the living human body is a riot of colour. The inside of a cadaver is all darkness. Grey like old steak.

'It's easy to get lost as you go,' the instructor said. 'Just use the bones as landmarks.'

Very dark inside.

&

It was a bright Sunday morning of early summer, promising heat, but with a fresh breeze blowing. Haven was thirteen. Aunt Mary was opening the house for spring and all the windows were raised. The lace curtains ballooned gently in and out of the window frames, hovering over the driveway and lawn, softly grazing Haven's arm. She was happy. She made a note of it. Wrote it down.

There.

&

Ken's hands were always cold in the mornings. It wasn't a problem for her at first. And then it was. And once it was a problem it just got bigger. Got under her and wouldn't go away.

&

It was like one of those scenes in a movie – it's all in slow motion suddenly and you know something's going to happen and you want to reach out and stop it from happening.

Chase remembered sitting in the car with his father at a gas station and a big eighteen-wheeler pulled in, a tanker, and so he was watching it, he would have been five probably, and the driver hopped down from the cab and then he turned and lifted down his son who was the same size as Chase, and he set him down on the ground carefully and looked around at the cars moving and then he took the boy's hand in his and walked slowly into the station, his head turning both ways, and then there was a car and the man reached down with his other hand and put it in front of his son's chest, you could see their breath, to stop him, when the car was still twenty feet away, and then he smiled and nodded at the driver who stopped and then he kept walking forward with his son. It was almost winter and the boy was wearing a coat unzipped and boots too big for him. The streaked windshield was so dirty it looked like it was covered with milk. Chase remembered thinking that his own father had never taken his hand even to cross a street and this was the moment that, like in a movie, he wished that he could stop from happening – the moment when he realized what was different, when it became true.

&

Heaven would be just the one moment, she thought, the best moment of your life, just played over and over, over and over. Hell would just be the opposite. That way you made them yourself.

&

It had been as if he were dancing, he later thought, dancing around the truth of it, around the smell of it. In offices and class-rooms where the kind and considerate ladies who smelled like mint or butterscotch were soft and quiet with him and listened to everything that he had to say and hovered, that was the word, hovered by him. Brought him snacks because he had no lunch, cupcakes from their lunches, a sweater because he had no coat.

'Look at those hands, would you like it if we went to wash you up?'

His hands in the warm water and the soap suds circling the sink in what must have been the staff room.

'How's that then, Chase … isn't that better? And what was it you were saying at recess about last night? When your father came home?'

'Nothing.'

He knew better. He took the snacks and the hovering. Knew when to be quiet. Just when to shut up.

'I don't remember.'

Kept them all.

and that's when I just 'cause it would be better not running down those leaves there could be sticks there would be better just and then in the classroom when we listened to that guitar music like that on the record turning and the lights out Haven says lights out and then the TV and the sounds you hear warm though moss on the rocks there's only a pulse in a thing if it's alive if not then that's it if you sleep on the ground you get a cold in your back in your bones 'cause your back remembers it remembers the cold and it won't go out of you, won't go out of you.

He did like to sit with his dad, though, while his dad listened to the ball game and drank his beer. Maybe there'd be some potato chips. Not take too many. It was good for the first few bottles. Chase would count the caps. One, two, three and then disappear. Eventually it was just one, then his father slurring already and swearing. Eventually Chase just stayed away. Heard who won at school the next day.

&

Haven joined the choir in Grade 5. It wasn't from any great love of music or even from any particular ability. She loved the church, loved being in the church, and joining the choir immediately tripled her time there because all practices were held at the church in the choir loft. They never went to church as a family except some years at Easter. When Mrs. Buckton asked on Mondays who had heard what Father had said at Mass the day before, Haven never put up her hand because people would know she was lying. God would know she was lying.

At the school mass each month their voices would float out over the heads of everyone below and at practice out over the echoing pews. Haven clasped her hands tight in front of her and took deep breaths between lines. Between hymns she could look down below to find the back of Chase's head.

There were wasps in between the stained-glass window in the choir loft and the sheet of Plexiglas that had been bolted in front of it on the outside to protect it from rocks or whatever might come its way. Haven had noticed them first as a low humming accompaniment to 'Companions on the Journey' and had turned her head slowly to see hundreds of them edging their way up under the yellow and blue cloak of an apostle. She imagined them finding their way out through a crack and destroying the mass by diving on the crowds of students and causing great consternation. When Father broke the bread they were still swarming safely behind glass. Haven liked the way that one of the teachers brought a gold cup full of the bread up to them while everyone else had to line up below. It felt like being in a restaurant. What she thought a restaurant would be like. That, and being up so high made her feel closer to God. She prayed that the wasps would not find their way free but they seemed to be stuck inside the window for good.

They almost never went to mass outside of school but Haven had liked being Catholic, had liked knowing people who knew the answers to things. She felt like she knew nothing about God or anything that was important and it had been good to know that somebody did.

&

The light from the blinds laid orange bands across her legs on one of the mornings that their parents had not come home, out somewhere in the long hurry and trail of alcohol, and she lay listening to Chase turn under the blankets and breathe in catches and starts. She prayed that the door of the trailer would not open and the voices would not start, tearing at each other or grinding away in sloppy happiness and in either case saying things she knew were not for her. She preferred to be forgotten from a distance.

She held her hands tightly together for a few moments. She was certain of it: one day she could be alive, like this, the scratchy blanket, the dust turning in the air … and the next day dead. She crawled over Chase to find a jar of peanut butter on the kitchen counter and sat licking peanut butter from a fork and looking out over the frozen grass and trees. If she could, she would live in a house made of crystal. The frost had etched long stretching patterns over the lawn.

She heard Chase in the hallway and began to look for bread.

At morning recess, Chase was standing watching some older boys, Todd Bickert and Wayne Scarff, drawing with chalk on the wall of the school. He knew that they shouldn't have been doing that, knew that he should probably not be standing there watching them, but he was unable to pull himself away. Recess was almost over and then he would be back inside with the coloured paper and scissors, with the wooden easels covered with years and years of effort with poster paint. The smell of the sticky glue congealing in the little baby food jars like pablum. Popsicle-stick spreaders. The rows of silver hooks, the tiled floor and the water fountain that made a high whistling sound when you leaned on the handle and made Mrs. Williams' voice even more edgy and thin and brittle sounding. With the lights off and lying on mats in the afternoon with a whirring fan turning slowly and clicking, turning and clicking.

The boys turned at the sound of the yard bell and saw him standing there. Todd, the bigger of the two boys, had bright red hair and a splash of freckles across his face that seemed to go angry and redder when he saw Chase.

'That's a picture of Mary, and she's a virgin.' He leaned in close to Chase's face, his voice becoming louder and more threatening. 'And you don't even know what that means, do you?'

'That's 'cause you're an idiot,' the other boy said.

The two boys laughed and ran away towards the door of the school, leaving Chase with his face hot and welling up quickly with silent tears for not knowing what he did wrong, why they were angry with him or what would happen next. His shorts were scratchy against his legs. The glass in the windows of the school doors had a grid of wire running through it in case it shattered.

There was a place at the corner of the wall where the bigger kids clapped the chalkboard erasers each night after the last bell and which was encased in thick layers of gummy dust, yellow and white, and there was so much sadness.

&

She kept staring at Ken until he had to look away. Her eyes were a wall she built carefully. Used it to tear people down. They always fell.

&

It took just a certain amount of alcohol to make him stop thinking. Knew just where the line was. Crossed it. Found himself in a field one morning and couldn't think how to get home. Looking up at the clouds nailed to the sky. Crossed it again that night.

He had a comic book under the bed. Haven still asleep. Archie and Jughead and Betty and Veronica read it again Ease off, Jug! You're gonna blow a gasket! Halloween soon and that was a time for candy rattling in your bag get a chocolate bar which kind Kit Kat or Four Flavours Bar Six

> Sweet Marie
> Big Turk
> Eat-More
> Oh Henry!

like sex must be the names keep it in your pocket go all gooey melted chocolate that time he kept an Eat-More all day had just a little at a time kept it in the wrapper and the paper melted into it yellow shining soft in your mouth coated then fold the rest back in the wrapper and when you're done stick it under the bed for later.

⅋

'You've been smoking.'

'I have not,' Haven said.

'You have.'

Aunt Mary had a way of knowing things that she had no way of knowing.

'Think of yourself and those cigarettes of yours as a nice joint of meat. And me as your cleaver.'

She made a chopping motion with a particularly grim expression.

That was that.

⅋

Haven had ways to make the truth hide temporarily. When there was bread she would hide it between the bed and the wall so that it would still be in the house when it was time to pack lunches in the morning before the bus came. Often there was nothing to put between the bread.

'Is there anything in it?' Chase asked.

'Not today.'

Hold the bread tightly and it doesn't show. Eat alone so no one knows. On days there was no bread they would stay home and watch the bus at the end of the driveway slow and then pick up speed.

On days when there was nothing at all, Haven would invent food. Toothpaste. Shaving cream. The berries from near the door that were supposed to be poison and which did make them sick but which did not kill them.

'We'll be all right,' she told Chase, told herself.

Much of Chase's silence could be a form of patience.
    Written by his teacher on his Grade 2 report card.

It was blasphemous of her to think that the Jesus on the cross next to the altar looked like a monkey. She knew that even at fourteen, that Aunt Mary would curse her for being a blasphemer, *Keep a civil tongue, for the love of Christ you're in Church …* They had started going as soon as they moved in with her.

'We'll get you heathens sorted out,' she told them.

Haven was excited finally to be going to church officially.

But it did look like a monkey, like some sort of grim scientific dissection gone wrong, all twisted up and nut brown, not like

Jesus meek and mild at all, the way she thought about Jesus, Jesus who walked on the water and calmed the storm.

Where in the name of God had they found this one?

It had never been there before and she couldn't be the only one sitting there on Palm Sunday thinking that it was more suited to a carnival tent than a Catholic altar. She was going to have to pass by it on the way to communion; perhaps it looked less like a simian closer up, less like some scene cut from *Planet of the Apes*. Surely everyone else was sitting there thinking the same thoughts – where had Father O'Keefe found it? Was the church forcing him to display it against his better judgment? Was it a directive from Rome? Was she the only one who would say something about this?

Probably.

Of course it would be wrong to talk about it. Not wrong to have it standing up there at the altar on a Sunday morning, mind you, just wrong to talk about it in the sunshine later.

She could already see Mary's hands turning white on the wheel.

'If you insist on talkin' this way, my miss, I would suggest that when you get home you sit yourself down by the telephone and randomly ring people until you find some poor unfortunate soul who is in any way interested in whatever the hell it is you're talkin' about because … because I'd like to assure you, Haven Katherine, that there is nobody in this vehicle who is.'

Then she would be silent for a while and then she would say something like, 'D'you know the Church has people who are experts about things like this?'

When Mary said *church* out loud it always had a capital C. You could hear the capital in her voice.

'And you are not one of them. And if you keep up with your blasphemin', the Lord will smite you. He'll crack you open like a walnut … '

Haven knew that she would say this or something very like it. Her bringing it up in the first place would really just be a test to see if she had the exact wording of what Mary would say. She knew that she would use the word *vehicle* for the dramatic effect, like using her middle name. 'Because I assure you, Haven Katherine, that there is nobody in this *vehicle* who is.'

Big deal.

She didn't care – it still looked like a monkey and nobody else would say it. It was just that kind of silence that got Him crucified in the first place and Aunt Mary's knuckles would just have to be white.

&

There was the time that the car engine woke him up. He looked out the window over his bed and saw the car in the driveway. He was careful not to wake Haven. He pulled on a sweater and went out in his pyjamas. His father was asleep and snoring with his head resting back on the seat. Chase turned the keys out of the ignition and turned off the headlights. He closed his father's door and stood looking for a while at his father's head sideways. Climbed into the back seat. Pulled his sweater tight.

&

The man lying cold and grey on the table would be known to Haven in ways that even his wife, his lovers, his children had never imagined. He would give up his secrets to her as if he were no more than a book, no more than a puzzle.

Prominent forehead.

Pale, freckled skin.

Large, sagging earlobes.

Hair in the nose and ears.

The mouth was contorted into what everyone referred to as a 'death scream.' Silent. Rigor mortis. It was more than just two words.

It was this.

Chronic obstructive pulmonary disease. The evidence: a barrel chest, blue-grey fingernails. Most of the body was covered with a series of white towels. Like hotel towels, Haven thought, small and thin. Dry. Insufficient.

One by one the group removed the towels and found, under the last, an orange plastic bracelet around the left ankle bearing the number 4327.

Well, hello, Haven thought. Hello, 4327.

&

Haven had once described Lucky to Chase as she had seen him one morning from the kitchen window. She had watched him run around in the backyard and then lie down on his back in the grass and stare up at the sky.

'Like he was praying … ' she told Chase.

'Dogs don't lie on their backs,' Chase said, 'unless they're rolling in shit.'

He had his own theology.

&

Haven wasn't home. It was the first thing that surfaced in Chase's mind as he awoke. That and the dream. He was out somewhere without his family, at some mall, and he needed to pee. Nobody would let him go pee, everyone wanted to keep looking at things in the stores, and when he finally found his way to the bathroom all of the urinals were sealed with a yellow tape so they wouldn't be used. Around the corner of the washroom he found a tiled shower which in the dream had made sense and had been such a relief. It had made sense, too, to take himself out and start peeing there in the shower, and he had needed to go so badly that it didn't really matter when it started going down his legs and getting his pants wet. He turned on the shower to wash away the pee. He wished his family was there and that he was not alone. Now his pants were all wet and then he woke up to think of Haven. Then he remembered that Haven was still in the hospital. That he was alone in the trailer with his parents. That it was winter and it was cold and that he had wet the bed. It must be time for school – without Haven, he couldn't be sure. Last time Haven had known what to do with the sheets, wrap them and keep them in his book bag so they wouldn't be found. Cover everything with the blanket. It would be dry by night. He had just begun when the door opened.

'The hell you doin' with your bed?' His father's voice like the cold on the window.

'It's nothing,' he remembered saying before the first blow took him on the back of his head and he fell to the floor. Then another to his ear that stung and rang and wouldn't stop ringing.

'Hurry up and get dressed, late for school.' And his father left.

It was sometimes sudden like that and sometimes there was a slow build-up – there were signs. Usually there was Haven there to read things for him. To interpret the quick rush of his father's anger, and his mother's silences. They had learned to be silent when she was silent.

He got dressed quickly. He would get to school and be safe. He stuffed the sheets at the bottom of his closet. His father had been drinking. Maybe he would forget about it and his mother would drive him to school. And Haven would be home soon.

He sat at the cold table and ate some toast that his mother had made. Nobody spoke of driving him to school. It had to be too late for the bus – it was usually Haven who woke up in time to get ready. The toast was dry ash in his mouth and his father sat staring at him over a cup of coffee.

'Little bastard,' he whispered, the words barely getting past his lips.

Chase chewed slowly, looking down.

'Who's gonna clean that up, eh?' he said louder.

Then, 'Little bastard,' again in a barely audible whisper.

Chase tried to take up less room at the table and kept his whole head down. Not chewing now, the toast a cold ball in his mouth.

Then the first hit, clearing the table and sending Chase crashing to the floor with his chair on top of him. Toast and plates, coffee. The sound of crashing just kept going and Chase felt himself being dragged down the carpet of the hallway and onto the smooth floor of the bathroom.

'Bastard,' he heard again, 'who's gonna clean that up?'

'I'm sorry,' Chase cried, and he was sorry, it wasn't right that he peed in his bed and made a mess and he would clean it up, wanted to tell his father that he would clean it up but he knew to be quiet, knew to say nothing and to just take the anger until it was gone.

'Who, who, who, eh?' the voice yelled, and with each word a blow to his head.

It had been like this before but it had always stopped. It always stopped by now. Haven always stopped it by now. Before now. He could hear the sound of the shower running and felt his face pushed up against the plastic shower curtain, could see his own blood red and streaming down the soft green plastic. Could hear the empty hollow sound of the shower and feel more blows to his back and his head. Started to feel empty and hollow like the sound of the shower and his father's voice echoed within him. He wondered where his mother was and then he saw her dress through the blood, passing by in the hall.

He felt himself being pushed into the shower stall and his pants tugging and ripping on the metal door frame.

'Who's gonna fuckin' clean that up?'

He would, he would clean it up if only …

'You're going to kill him, Jack.' His mother's voice quietly through the stinging cold water.

He tucked himself as closely in as he could on the floor of the stall and watched the water swirl red. Could feel the dull thuds against the side of his head. The boom and buckle of the metal walls of the shower stall.

I'm going down the drain, he thought.

Haven won't know where to find me.

And then it stopped.

He lay quiet with the water pouring onto him still and his arms and legs shaking. He wouldn't open his eyes yet. His parents had left. He opened his eyes slowly in a peek and found that one wouldn't open and that the other was covered with a film of red. He had to get to school where he would be safe. Haven would be home soon. She couldn't stay at the hospital forever.

When he crawled over to the sink and pulled himself up at the mirror, it was someone else in the reflection. Someone whose face was large and swollen, whose eyes were pushed apart by a nose twice the size of normal, whose wet hair dangled over a fore-head turning purple as he watched it. The rest of his life he remembered the thought that came next: that he wouldn't be able to go to school.

That, and the voice that had said softly, 'You're going to kill him, Jack.'

Like a ghost passing.

Chase opened his eyes.

Beautiful.

Ivy was standing by the window in her bike shorts looking out at the grey city and judging the weather. Then her eyes closed. Then opened. Her arms folded. Her hair. The smell of fresh coffee.

Chase looking around the room, everything still there. Closed his eyes. Deep breath. Sound of water. Warm. And the day ahead and waiting. Beautiful.

Haven loved to go swimming, which she did because within the trailer park there was a little pool and she didn't need permission or parents or anyone to take her there. She loved to be under the water and loved to feel the cold shock of the first dive. And under the water nobody could hear her screaming. She could open her mouth wide enough to encompass all of the unfairness and then bite it off at the end like the tail of a great snake, a long snake like the ones on TV that wrapped their twisting bodies around people and devoured them whole, one long gulp at a time. She could toss her head and cry and the pool water would swallow all the tears she could supply so that Chase would not say,

'What?'

and pull on her arm until she told him, yelling,

'Because it's not supposed to be like this, all right?' turning on him in the little lane leading between the trailers, the anger of the pool water returning, the two of them wrapped in bath towels and leaking wet grey footprints onto the concrete. 'Don't you know that? We're not supposed to be thinking of ways to stay away from home for longer, we're supposed to want to be

81

there. And I'm not supposed to be making your goddamn dinner every night.'

All of it coming out of her and at him suddenly.

She walked away from him.

'Nobody asked you,' he said defiantly, tears starting.

'Nobody had to,' she yelled, turning. 'Nobody's going to do it unless I do it … Nobody,' she added more softly, seeing his face, his arms folded against her, feet planted.

'We'll just sit there and starve if I don't … Nobody … Just let's just go,' she said weakly, reaching to pull at his towel, aware of the windows around them. 'C'mon, let's go.'

Pulling at his arm not to hurt him but to move him away from where anyone could see.

See how hurt he was already.

&

Stood pretty much outside of everything his whole life. And all the time listening. Trying to figure it out. Why he felt the way he did.

&

In winter it was a struggle just to get out the door. The walkway and steps were never shovelled.

'Are you not shovellin' the step?'

'It'll melt in the spring.'

Some mornings they would both have to apply their full weight to the screen door to push it against the new drift, more and more difficult as the snow became more compacted. One morning the whole door bent off the upper hinge, the lower hinge safely buried in the snow. They watched from the bus window, pulling away from a house that looked as if it had been attacked by a giant.

One thing their father had done was to build what he called a porch, really it was a roof, by the back door. Two timbers stood to carry a wooden wedge of boards that hung precariously over the step. As the winter progressed, the whole structure sagged and complained of the weight, and you couldn't escape the thought that coming in or going out one day there would be a catastrophe, that the whole thing would give up the ghost in the snow and crash down, killing whoever was going in or coming out. Haven reasoned that it would be the second person in line who would suffer. The first to go through would have time to duck out of the way at the start of the groaning sound that would signal the collapse. The slam or the opening of the door would have triggered the avalanche, and by the time it had built to fever pitch and rained the icy wooden death blow, it would be the second head in line to take the hit. Some days she was noble and said, 'After you … ' to Chase with a hesitant and repentant eye to the plywood heavens as she followed. If she was mad at Chase or at the world, she would slip through first and slam the door so that there would be ample time as he swore at her and struggled with the handle. She always snuck in or out ahead of her father even if she risked getting a slap to the head.

He built it. Let it fall on him.

'He'll kill me,' Chase said quietly.

'No he won't,' Haven said, slowly spreading her hands out on her knees palms down, looking at them. 'I won't let him.'

Two

The things that took place during the day

'No,' she said.

She held him tighter and she looked into his eyes for a moment. *If we stay like this,* Haven thought.

'No, it's all right ... ' she told him again.

If we stay like this, it will be all right. We will be okay.
If we stay like this ...
we can stay like this.

&

Dairy Queen. Soft-serve, medium. Because it was perfect. Because it was pure and white and creamy and it was the same every time. Cardboard box of a cone holding it all up. Big cold steel machine. Little paper wrapper. Licking around the edge so it didn't drip or just letting it drip down over her fingers in the hot afternoon sun because nobody would tell her not to. It was freedom and happiness for $1.43.

And it was the same every time. Kept all of the wrappers in a drawer in the kitchen. Because there was nobody left to tell her not to do that either.

&

Not safe, she knew that right away. They played the game on Bent Mile Road, which was just past the forest of trees in back of the trailer park. It was a concession road made of gravel with split-rail fences and cedar scrub lining both sides. Dry and dusty. They were playing with Tommy, who was visiting his grandparents in one of the trailers. He was from Toronto where he lived in an apartment in a tall building. It had been Tommy's idea but Chase had taken to it right away. Haven had been less sure.

86

'C'mon,' Chase told her, 'it's fun.'

'You've never done it.' She was unsure of situations where she did not take the lead.

'I know, but it sounds like fun. You scared?' he asked.

'No.'

They toiled through the weeded gully by the fence and climbed over the mossy logs, pulling at the rusted wire and the dried vines that caught at their clothes. They slouched out of the sheltered shade and into the gravel-edged sun as if they belonged there by the side of the road. There were little bugs in the air.

'This is a good spot,' Tommy said.

'How do you know?' Haven asked. Tommy was from Toronto – how would he know anything about good spots on roads like this?

'It just is,' Tommy replied with certainty.

'C'mon,' Chase said.

They crouched down in the scratchy weeds and waited.

'Who's first?' Tommy asked.

'You are,' Haven told him, pulling at her skirt and shifting her weight.

'Why?'

'So if you get killed we can still go home.'

What she really meant was that if Tommy was run over she would still have Chase and he would still have her. She said only, 'We're having spaghetti tonight.'

'Rock paper scissors?' Chase suggested.

'Okay,' said Tommy.

She and Chase both threw rock and Tommy threw paper so she and Chase threw again. She knew that Chase would throw rock again so she threw scissors.

'That's you,' declared Tommy, 'you're up.'

'I know that.'

'So c'mon.'

It would occur to Haven later in her life that the reason for her growing anger and frustration over the deadly game had been that it was just that, a game.

'This is a stupid game,' she said.

'You had scissors,' Tommy insisted.

'We could do something else,' Chase relented, sensing now his sister's frustration and reading it as fear.

'No,' Haven said, staring Tommy down.

'Okay then,' Tommy said.

Okay then, okay then, Haven repeated in her head as she lay waiting in the weeds by the edge of the gravel. Chase and Tommy had retreated to the protection of the fence line – she could hear their muffled voices through the branches. *Okay then.* She flicked her leg at a trespassing fly and looked uneasily down the road. She could hear a car somewhere but wasn't sure how far away it was or in which direction it was headed.

'Car!' Tommy called.

Haven could see the rising dust as she peered out between the weeds and heard the growing sound of the crunching gravel, the noise of the engine as the car bore down. The bright glint of sun off the chrome fender.

'Go!' she heard Tommy yell.

'Go!'

Something kept her until the last possible moment and then she flew into the road, her shoes kicking the gravel behind her, loose footing almost dropping her, and propelling her before the oncoming car much closer than she had anticipated. She could feel the air sucked from around her as the car passed; the horn blared indignantly in a long and angry whine that stopped as the wheels skidded in the loose stone and the driver struggled to keep control of the vehicle. Her eyes snapped shut as she imagined the car rolling off the road, just as she herself was thrown headlong into the opposite ditch, where she tumbled, felt the painful snap of her breath knocked out of her, regained her feet once more and hurdled herself in one jump over the broken fence and into the cedars, which scratched at her face and arms. She fell again and lay with her head next to a large rock. She could hear nothing from the road. She could see a ladybug slowly making its quiet way along the mossy surface of the stone, down into each shaded ravine-like crack and up again with a silent determination. She looked back through the trees and saw the dust still sweeping in a wave down the road. Then she heard the car door slam and the feet running on the gravel and she was up again and running through the trees along the fence line and then out into the field and through the corn.

'Gonna get yourself killed!' she heard a voice yelling and knew she was safe then because if the man was taking the time to yell out it meant he had already given up the chase.

She kept running.

When she finally met up with Chase and Tommy back on the other side, she refused to let Chase try on the pretext that they were already late for supper. Chase was indignant, partly because supper was unlikely to be ready unless Haven had run home and prepared it, but the look in Haven's eyes and the tone of her voice let him know that it was final, and Tommy had not argued. She knew that he had seen how close she had come and that he would be unable to match her run. She knew also that she spoke with the authority of the almost-but-not-quite killed.

'We'll play tomorrow,' she told them.

But they didn't, and soon Tommy went back to Toronto and they never played again.

And so she had saved Chase that time.

&

The summer she was fourteen, Haven started making cardboard signs and standing out by the highway in front of the house they had moved into with Mary.

'What's she playing at now?' Mary would ask, wiping her hands at the kitchen window.

Chase took a look. 'She's not happy,' he offered.

Mary gave him the eyeball. 'Is that right?'

'She's a girl … ' he tried.

'She'd better get used to it,' Mary said, still squinting out the little window.

Haven tore cardboard from boxes and used the heavy black markers that squeaked when you used them and smelled to high heaven. Then she'd choose a sign that felt right and stand by the road for hours swatting at the mosquitoes and flies. Watching the caterpillars struggle over the gravel at her feet.

New York City.
Miami.
Brazil.
Paris.
Tibet.
Away From Here.

Swatted at the mosquitoes and wiped the sweat from her brow. Chase watched her from the window, and once he brought her a glass of ice water, beads of condensation running down the sides and darkening the earth at their feet.

'Where are you going today, Haven?' he'd ask.

Nowhere.

&

After it had become apparent that Ken was never coming back and that her marriage was really, officially over, Haven and Chase both ended up at Mary's house for a cup of tea – or to watch Mary have a cup of tea while they sipped coffee from Tim Horton's. Mary wouldn't allow a coffee machine in the house.

'I'm hungry,' April said.

'I've left med school,' Haven announced. It was as good a time as any. 'I'm not going to do medicine anymore … '

Mary looked across the table at her. 'Your husband has left you and you've left school and now left medicine altogether, not just trying to be a doctor but all of medicine, have I got that right? So that's a no to that whole idea of medicine. Have I got that right now?'

Haven nodded. 'Yes,' she said, adding, 'I'm sorry.'

'Sorry? Should I ring the papers to alert them that your life's headed down the crapper?'

'I'm just telling you,' Haven said.

'You're just telling me? So no call to the *Globe and* friggin' *Mail* then? Christ. Mary looked into her tea cup, then at the wall for what seemed like a full minute, then back to her tea cup, then back to Haven. 'What else are you just telling me? You've decided to put April up for adoption? Selling her to a childless couple for the rent money?'

Haven closed her eyes and waited. Chase absentmindedly played with his takeout cup, taking the plastic lid off and tearing at it slowly.

'Will the two of you move in here then?' Mary asked.

'No.'

'You're welcome to, you know.'

'I know.' Haven got up to make a sandwich for April.

'Well then.'

'Thank you. Thanks, Mary.' Haven looked briefly at April reading a book at the table. 'But we're fine.'

'I know you're fine.'

'I'm going to become a teacher.'

Mary got up to help with the food. 'Well, there's worse things than that … '

Haven took the jam from the fridge.

'Hey,' Chase said, 'I won a muffin!' He held out his cup and showed it to April.

'Can I have it?' she asked.

'Sure.'

'I'm making you a sandwich, April,' Haven said.

'Yeah,' April said, not looking up at her. Nose back into the book.

Chase began to rip the rolled-up rim off the cup.

'End of a marriage is the beginning of something else,' Mary said. 'Who knows what … ' She reached for a loaf of bread in the cupboard, hefting her large frame up onto her toes.

'When I married Francis,' she said with a grunt, 'it was all hearts and flowers.' She took the jam from Haven. 'Then back to the hotel, and it was all arses and elbows.' She finished making April's sandwich. 'Then we're off to Ireland and then Francis is gone to cancer and I'm back in Canada for the two of you, and this one … '

She looked down at April and then up at Haven. Haven looked at April's sandwich. Mary had trimmed off the crusts.

'You'll be just fine,' Mary said.

She washed up the knife using the rubber hose and shower-head she had used to wash their hair with in the kitchen sink when they were kids.

'I know,' Haven said.

'And I'm sorry that I wasn't here, Haven, when you were grow-ing up. I am sorry about that.'

'I know.'

'But did you know that my Francis had one arm longer than the other?' Mary asked, turning the air of the room warmer. 'Did you know that? Did I tell you what folks in Ireland used to call him? The Clock.' She laughed and shook her head, looking out the window over the sink. She held one arm short to her side and made clock movements.

Lately Mary had been telling them all the stories she had already told them years before, as if she were dusting off an old box of photos and pulling them out again. They had all gotten tired of telling her that they'd already heard them before. And they really didn't mind hearing them again.

Haven placed the sandwich down carefully in front of April. Chase reached for Haven's hand and held it for a moment.

'And my grandfather, now they used to call him ... Did I tell you? The Moth – d'you know why they did that? Called him the Moth? He used to stop for a drink at every light on the way home – did I ever tell you that?' She looked at Haven.

'I don't think so,' Haven told her. But she had. Just last week.

'Yeah,' she said. 'There's worse things than losing your husband. It didn't kill me ... and it won't kill you either.'

Haven looked at Chase and then took her hand away. She wanted to cry. But she didn't.

It was the day before Chase's seventh birthday. He was hoping for a hockey stick with the Canadiens logo. With maybe a net to shoot against. He was in the bathroom and he heard his father swearing in the living room. He knew that his mother had asked for the bookcase she had bought to be put together before she got home. He could hear the swearing and the metal sound of the tools and the shelves. Then he could hear his father walking around and swearing more and then he couldn't hear anything else for a while. He moved closer to the door. Then he heard the godalmighty sound of the whole thing crashing to the floor. It sounded like the roof coming down. He knew the bookcase was pretty big from the picture on the box that had been sitting in the middle of the living room for the last week.

'We don't have that many books,' his father had said suddenly in the middle of a hockey game.

'It's not just for books, Jack,' his mother had said a couple of minutes later.

Montreal scored.

'That's more like it,' his father said and opened another beer.

'Sure, but it's mostly for books,' he said, 'books and other shit.' He eyed the box from across the room. 'We don't have that many books. Nobody's got that many books … '

His mother lit a cigarette. 'People do,' she said.

It didn't sound too good out there now. Haven was in the bedroom. He could hear sounds like his father was jumping up and down on the shelves and kicking them. He opened the door a crack to see if he could see Haven. She was standing in their bedroom door looking down the hallway. She shook her head no when she saw him.

Then the sounds stopped and his father swore a few more times. 'Fucking goddamned piece of Sears shit … '

Haven nodded then and they went together down to the end of the hall and peered into the living room. The metal shelves were all over the place and bent. The TV was knocked over.

In the middle of the floor their father sat still holding a pair of pliers in one hand. When he looked over at them standing in the doorway, Haven stiffened, but then he started to laugh.

'How's it look?' he asked. 'Good?'

And Chase started to laugh too. It seemed like the safest thing to do.

'Go on, bring out some fuckin' books – it's ready … '

But he was kidding. It was safe now. They could breathe.

But Chase never got the hockey stick. Never got the net.

&

Goodbye to medicine then. Hello to teaching. Simple. It turned out teaching was the thing she wanted to do after all. It was how she could fix things. Little things. She could fix little things. Here, let me show you how to do this fraction. It's not cancer. But I do know how to fix it. And I can show you. Let me show you how.

And April was eleven. And no dad. But life went on. April had Chase. Chase could be April's dad now.

&

Ivy was painting her toenails. Her leg up. Her foot on the sink. Striped cotton. The lace edge scooped down and around. She looked up into the mirror.

'What?'

Chase told her that he loved her. Just like that.

He saved her, though. He walked away.

&

She couldn't stand the dirt anymore. And no one should have to be quiet all day. She knew that he was asleep. She knew that they weren't allowed to make noise. For God's sake keep the children quiet for an hour Jesus my head. She just wanted to have it done. It was the middle of the afternoon and she should be allowed to vacuum if the trailer needed to be vacuumed. And it did. There was no point in putting it off and she just wanted to have it done. She knew he was asleep. She did it anyway.

95

'What are you doing?' Chase asked.

'This is a vacuum cleaner. I'm going to clean this carpet because I can't remember the last time I cleaned it.'

Chase watched her bang around with the hose and pull the dresser away from the wall to plug the vacuum in.

'Dad's asleep,' he said.

Haven flipped on the switch with her foot and started rolling the vacuum over the carpet, pushing at the rolled-up pants and socks on the floor. Chase pulled his legs up to the end of the bed and sat watching. Haven pushed the vacuum under the bed, listening to it suck up plastic soldiers, marbles, hair barrettes. Listened to them rattle through the hose smaller and smaller.

'Haven ... '

She knew it from his face before she turned to see her father coming through the door in his underwear. Chase's face white.

'For Chrissake trying to sleep!' he yelled. He was trying to get at her but the dresser with the mirror on the back was in the way.

'It's dirty,' she yelled, knowing he couldn't get at her yet but that he would and not caring anyway, just angry and lifting the hose up towards him to keep his hands away.

'Dammit,' he yelled at her and at the dresser and he punched at the back of the mirror in his way once, twice and harder and the mirror cracked and she saw him grab both sides and pull it off the dresser and she saw him throwing it down at the floor, at her, and she tried to back up out of the way and she saw her father's face receding back through the door and all she could hear was the sound of the vacuum she had dropped the hose and she looked down to find it to find her leg opened up by the mirror and her one foot hanging limp and the red blood coming from it like a garden hose it was her blood and the sound of the vacuum and she hopped on one foot and lifted her leg and the foot just dangling and the red and she had to get to the bathroom if she got to the bathroom it would be all right the red could go on the tile floor where she could clean it because it would never come out of this carpet and Chase was grabbing her and the sound of the vacuum and trying to get around the dresser holding her leg and she was saying to Chase that she had to get to the bathroom help me get to the bathroom I have to get to the bathroom Chase I'm bleeding and Chase was helping her get past the dresser and hold her foot up hold her leg up and all the blood that kept going in the hallway on the wall and how was she going to stop it if she could get to the sink and lift her leg up into the sink and run the water to clean it and she could hear her father yelling still *Shit Shit Shit* and he was in the bathroom already looking at his hand and Chase was telling her to sit down What? Just sit down now Haven Sit down on the ground! Sit down! and the carpet more blood on the carpet the way that mirror just exploded and Chase had a towel or something and he was wrapping it around her leg but that wouldn't be clean that wouldn't be clean Chase if she could get to the sink or the shower but her father was in the bathroom big in the bathroom swearing and looking at his hand in the sink Chase was looking at her grey-white in the face and wrapping the towel tighter and tighter looking down at the red and then she looked up and away and the perforated tiles in the ceiling lighter and lighter and lighter and lighter and that was it. Quiet.

That time he saw those two boys. He was driving around in the Jeep and he saw two boys carrying a box through a field. It looked like they didn't have a care in the world. They had something in their box and they were taking it somewhere, or it was empty maybe and they were going to fill it up. It didn't matter. They were just walking through the field in the sun. Like nothing in the world could ever hurt them.

&

Keep it up in the air so the blood stops. Like a series of photographs she remembered it. She heard Chase on the phone talking about an ambulance. Her leg in front of her wet in the towel. It didn't hurt. Hold it up. Keep it up. Her father going down the hall past her. The ambulance men talking to Chase. Sitting up on the stretcher being carried into the sunlight. Her mother upside down with her hand in her hair. The neighbours watching. Looking up and the trees going past. The men asking questions.

Do you have any allergies to medication?

Her mother's face.

Chase.

&

Chase pictured it once like a big caravan. God driving a big creaking wooden wagon and wearing that big purple coat that a God would wear and reaching down his hand to Chase and saying, 'C'mon, take a seat up here … '

In the big creaky wooden wagon. The low-hanging branches of the trees at the edge of the evening field and a voice somewhere singing softly. Fireflies and evening moths by the lanterns of the caravan. 'C'mon up, take your seat … '

And pulling him right up. Right up into the seat and then the caravan moving on.

&

'Tell us again. Just explain to us once more what happened.'

'I did.'

'Just once more.'

'My brother threw a ball at the mirror and it broke and it cut my leg.'

'And he was throwing the ball at you?'

'That's right.'

'Because you were making noise with the vacuum?'

'He didn't mean to hurt me.'

'And is that right, son?'

'Yes.'

'Yes?'

'That's right.'

The policemen looking at each other. Chase and Haven sat looking at each other.

'You're sure about this? That thing cut right through your artery, you know. Hadn't been for that towel you could've bled to death before any real help got there … '

They glanced at each other again. 'You're sure?'

'Yes.'

'And if we went back there we'd find that ball?'

'Yes,' Haven answered. 'It's red with a white stripe.'

Details were important. People believed details.

You didn't believe me I told you this would happen I did I said it was going going goinggoinggoing to be like this is the way that things happen the way in which things like this happen one thing happens and then another happens just like that something is and then it isn't there is no is and isn't there just is is is and there isn't anything that isn't isn't anything that isn't which isn't everything is it just is is is there just is and there isn't any isn't isn't any isn't and there never was world without end amen

isn't anything you can do about it it just is

that's right

&

'Yes?'

She always answered the phone with a *yes* rather than a *hello*. There were so few people who called her that *hello* seemed unnecessary. It was Chase or Mary or April or it was someone she didn't want to talk to.

'Haven?'

'Yes, Mary, it's me … '

There was the sound in Mary's voice again, sounding more like a child than a great-aunt or a grandmother. 'Haven, I … '

'Yes, Mary?'

There was something wrong.

'I can't find the cookies I put into the oven.'

Haven wrapped the phone cord in her hand. 'You can't find them?' she asked.

'I put them in the oven … and they're not there now, I can't think where they've gone. I … '

Haven closed her eyes and pulled on the cord. 'It's okay, Mary.' Haven could hear the fear in Mary's voice. Tried to keep it out of her own. 'I'll come over and we'll find them.'

'I … '

'Don't worry.'

Haven told herself while driving that they'd just find the cookies on top of the fridge or someplace like that and they'd have a laugh and a tea and that would be the end of it. But she knew – there'd been too many things lately, she knew it would not be the end of it. She knew then that it was something beginning and not ending. A cloud just getting bigger.

They searched the kitchen and the rest of the house and found nothing. Haven switched off the oven, making a note, in spite of herself, that Mary had neglected to do this. It would have been on almost two hours now with no cookies.

'The Case of the Missing Cookies,' she said, trying to make it sound like the title of one of the Encyclopedia Brown books her students read.

Then she thought about the action of leaning over to put cookies in the oven and she went to each bedroom in turn, finding the pan of dough under what used to be her bed. She stood in the middle of the room with the pan in her hand, not sure what to do next. Then Mary walked in.

'Found them,' Haven told her. She made herself smile.

Mary stared at the pan.

'They were under the bed,' Haven explained weakly.

'Well,' Mary said, still staring hard at the pan as if it were a magic trick. 'That's funny.'

But it wasn't. And neither one of them laughed.

He couldn't remember his line. Chase was standing in his bathrobe at the side of a polished wood stage behind an enormous thick red curtain, a wise man waiting. Big yellow star made out of bristol board. Lambs painted on big sheets of brown paper. It had taken a week just to make all the lambs. Soon he would have to walk out on the stage. Everyone would see him.

'We follow the star!' That was it.

Haven still swam, as an adult, in the same way that she had as a child – for the purpose of screaming underwater so that no one would know.

It was her privacy and comfort. And the swimming was good for her – it toned her body and disciplined her mind. It allowed her, with each length of the pool, to realign the thoughts that her mind followed with who she wanted to be, with what she wanted to be thinking about. She pulled at the bottom of her wet suit in the change room, examined her red-rimmed chemical eyes in the cold light of the mirror. I look like I've been crying, she thought, crying and up all night long. I look like I've been screaming.

&

You weren't where you were when you were reading. You were somewhere else. There was a book about a tiny Indian who lived in a boy's closet. There was one about a family of children who had a tunnel that led to another world. One about the Bobbsey twins and an old house with a closet with a secret passage. One about a boy who found a passage that took him into a place with a magic little car and a toll booth. But mainly there was the book about the children who find a closet full of coats and behind the coats there is no back wall but a whole other world full of magic.

When they lived in the trailer she kept that book under the mattress of their bed and lived in the fear that someone from the school library would someday ask her about it but no one ever did. Brown bumpy cover that felt like Braille when she closed her eyes and ran her fingertips across it. Little black silhouettes of the children on the spine, which always made her feel a little creepy, like they were dead then pressed flat and preserved just under the surface of the leather.

It was one of the few things she carried into the new house with her, scrambled in a cardboard box with her clothes and her things from school and from the shelter.

'Look at the pair of you,' Mary had said, watching them up the walk to the door, 'like the crew off a sunk boat.'

It was the first time they had their own rooms, and they spent the first months still together in one room.

'Time to break it up,' Mary announced one day at lunch. 'You two are getting too old to be with yourselves like that.'

'Like what?' Haven had cut back.

'Like … ' Mary took a breath, 'like toast and jam – you're never one without the other. I don't have to be the only soul on the planet with just a pillow for company, do I?'

So they split up, sometime around starting high school, and that's when Haven started to dig her way into the soft plaster of the closet wall. She'd close herself up in the closet dark with a book and a flashlight. There was a hole in the plaster and she'd pull and scrape at it absentmindedly like a scab as she read. This is what it's like being an adult, she thought, it's being alone.

It all came to Haven: the contents of the trailer and all of her mother's clothes. There wasn't much to show for it all. Not much to show. She took it all over to Chase's in boxes. A pair of her father's shoes. A hairbrush. A phone. A few cassette tapes they couldn't play because Chase didn't have a player.

'I thought you had one,' she said.

'There's one in the Jeep but it's busted.'

A wind-up alarm clock.

A frying pan and some cutlery in a cardboard box.

There was a bracelet of her mother's. Her parents hadn't owned the appliances. The furniture wasn't worth keeping.

A pair of earrings that she had kept. Just simple silver ovals. When you placed them on a table they looked like two little sailboats gliding on the water.

She wanted to give it all away at first: the clothes to the Goodwill and the rest to the Sally Ann, but she just couldn't do it. They took the two boxes out to the back of the property behind the house where Chase was renting the basement apartment and they dropped them into the creek from Chase's canoe.

'They'll sink,' Chase said.

But they didn't, at least not right away, and then finally they did but for days afterwards his mother's dresses would float, one by one, to the surface and catch in the weeds by the bank. He never told Haven. Just went out to the creek with a paddle each day and pushed them along downstream. Chase kept nothing.

Mary thought the place she was living now was okay. She didn't understand why she couldn't live at home anymore. She liked the ice cream – strawberry the best, though vanilla and chocolate were fine too, liked to mash it up in the bowl, stir it around until it was like cold soup. They let her walk down to the cafeteria now and she would take the elevator down in her bathrobe and with cold ankles and wait in line for a bowl and take it to one of the tables by the windows to watch the shifting patterns of light across the lawn, the trees and the street, and sometimes she would meet someone there and strike up a conversation and this made her feel better, this small amount of control over things, this freedom. Haven and Chase would come and see her, and April. She remembered them. She could see them now.

'I've been meaning to call you,' Chase told Haven.

'Sure you have,' she answered, smiling at him and closing her car door.

'I wanted to tell you I found some work gloves for you.'

'This is Ken,' she said.

There was a guy getting out of the other side of the car.

'Ken,' he said, offering his hand.

'Sure … yeah, Chase,' Chase said.

Nothing happened then and they stood in the driveway looking at each other and Haven said, 'Ken said he wouldn't mind giving us a hand with the wood.'

Chase was renting a basement apartment in a bungalow on Clothier and the lady who owned it had ordered three cords of wood that sat heaped in a pile in the side yard.

'Great,' Chase said, pretending to be easygoing. He didn't like having to talk about something, having to readjust his thinking about how things would go and pretending it was okay at the same time. It felt like juggling something. Felt like something would fall.

'Great,' he said again.

They started stacking the wood into neat rows the way the lady wanted it. Chase gave the work gloves to Haven and Ken said he didn't need any. Chase was worried that they wouldn't have room to put all the wood the way the lady wanted. Then Haven said, 'You know what, you guys don't need me – I'm going to run get some groceries and I'll bring back some coffee.'

Chase could tell what she was doing. She was handing the work gloves to Ken. She was backing out of the driveway. She was trying to get him to like Ken.

'So, Haven tells me you do some art,' Ken said, putting on the gloves.

Chase could tell he was a nice enough guy, in a way. He heard quotation marks around the word *art*. Nice enough guy in a way, but it wasn't Chase's way. He didn't like new people until after they weren't new anymore. That was from experience. It was something he had learned. Most people didn't make it past new.

'Make any money with it?' Ken asked.

Not going to work, Chase knew. There wasn't enough there to like.

&

Can't. Try again. And then. And then. And then. Nothing. She tried. Her name was Mary. Mary. That was her name.

&

He could never explain why most people didn't make any sense to him. What could he tell Haven that would be something she wanted to hear and also the truth? There was no way. Chase sat on top of the wood pile brushing little pieces of wood from his gloves. Ken was having a cigarette. Ken had stopped talking a while back. Chase had made sure of that.

'You think he's an asshole,' Haven said after Ken had left.

Chase thought about what to say. 'He doesn't mean to be,' he offered.

&

Everything ends sadly. Everything comes undone. It was expensive to keep Mary in the home. It was what had to be done. It wasn't safe for her to live alone. Haven had tried moving back in with her to watch over her but she had to go to work and Mary had nearly burned down the house with the iron. April had been sleeping upstairs. No. It was what had to be done. It was the best they could do. She and April stayed in the house and all the money went to pay for the home. Chase couldn't help. There was nothing that Chase could do. Mary had to be safe.

&

His father had one movie that he liked to watch every time it was on. Watched it over and over, drunk and sober. Watched that movie and the Canadiens. Someone asked him once why he was a Montreal fan when he was Irish.

'Fight the fuckin' English,' Chase remembered him saying. 'That's all I'm sayin' … '

Watched that movie whether it was on in the morning or late at night. It was *Rio Grande* with John Wayne. The Duke, his father said. He'd watch anything with John Wayne in it, but that one was his favourite. Chase would move into the living room without making any noise and watch it with him. Once it was on in the afternoon and Chase was supposed to be in bed with the flu but he snuck in and watched and halfway through his father noticed he was there but he didn't say anything or make him go back to bed.

John Wayne was a guy in the cavalry fighting with the Indians and there was this young guy who was his son. He was in the cavalry too but it seemed like John Wayne and his wife didn't want him in the cavalry. They fought with each other but John Wayne was proud of his son, you could tell. Even though he never said anything about it. Chase didn't remember too much else about the movie. Years later he'd seen it in the video store. It wasn't on

TV much anymore. He picked it up at the video store and read the back, which didn't say anything about a son, just John Wayne and Maureen O'Hara and fighting Indians. He started to wonder if he'd made up the whole thing about the son even being in the movie. Then one time he rented it just to see. But he never ended up watching it. It just sat there on top of the television. Built up twenty dollars in late fees.

&

She heard that her father was dead on a bright January afternoon. It was Saturday. April was at dance class. The coldest day in ten years, the radio had just finished saying when the phone rang. Mary just told her outright.

'Haven, your father's dead.' Before even a hello.

'It's best just to say some things without a lot of movin' around them first,' she explained. 'I could've eased you up to it but at the end of it he's still just as dead. Anyway, he's dead, and I'm sorry. I'm sorry for your troubles.'

'How do you know?'

Haven's own voice sounded suddenly like a child's to her as she stood in the kitchen, her hand wrapped in the phone cord.

'The police called. It was a heart attack, there'll be no ... '

Thank god.

'There'll be no funeral.'

'Thanks for calling, Mary.'

'I'll be over later.'

'Okay, bye.'

She walked into the living room and sat on the cold couch, watched the snow fall and had a cup of tea. His heart had failed so long before, she thought, so long before this cold day had seen fit to take the rest of him. She called Chase but there was no answer. She didn't leave a message. Nobody needs a message like that. She made another cup of tea and stood again by the window. She thought of April dancing in front of the big mirror at the Legion where the dance class was held. After a time she felt slightly lightheaded, felt as if she were rising into the air, and had to look down to be certain her feet were still on the floor.

&

'You know the funny thing about country songs?' his father had asked him once.

'What?'

They were driving to pick up some beer and listening to the radio. The sun was bright through the grey windshield and Chase felt a little sick.

'Fella's always singing about a girl, right?'

'Yes.' Chase didn't know for sure if he knew any country songs.

His father looked in the rear-view. 'Only the girl's never there,' he said. He lit another cigarette. 'Girl's always gone,' he said again to make his point. And he laughed.

'Can we get some ice cream?' Chase asked.

'Maybe.'

That meant no.

&

Many questions will arise relating to the death or injury of a loved one. The questions pertain to the circumstances leading up to or surrounding death or injury, or pertain to the possibility of emotional or physical pain suffered by the individual. The forensic pathologist is capable of offering an expert opinion when considering the severity and duration of pain. If the death was not witnessed, the opinion should be in the form of a 'range of time' unless it is clear that the death occurred suddenly. The range is narrow or broad depending on the specific circumstances. The nature and extent of the injury or injuries will obviously affect the degree and duration of pain and suffering.

&

Mary was comparing winter temperatures to those of her childhood. 'My grandfather passed in the coldest February in one hundred years,' she said, spreading jam on a piece of toast.

'He passed?' Haven asked.

'Died.'

Haven chose a piece of toast from the plate and scraped the darker patches with her thumbnail. Every morning there was oatmeal and toast and jam. There was always milk in the fridge. You didn't have to smell it first. On the weekend there were fried eggs or pancakes with syrup. Bacon.

'It was February and the ground was too hard to break,' Aunt Mary said.

The black crumbs collected under Haven's nail.

'Too hard to what?' Chase asked.

'Couldn't make a hole for the poor man to be dead in,' Mary said.

Chase spooned his oatmeal.

Mary looked at him for a moment. 'So we put him on the porch for the winter.'

Haven and Chase looked at each other, wide-eyed.

'Just sitting there?' Haven asked.

'Of course not just sitting there!' Mary exploded. 'He was in his pine box.'

She cleaned away the plates and set about cleaning them. Steam rose from the sink.

'Every morning we'd say "Bye, Grandpa" when we made our way to school – that'd be your great-grandad. You take after him you two – you're a quiet lot.'

Haven and Chase looked at each other again.

&

A ninety-three-page course syllabus. A corpse and a table. Some very sharp instruments. For gaining access to the truth. A four-teen-day journey through the human body. All the stops along the way. Haven opened her book. Began.

&

It sat like a small coffin of polished wood and glowing tubes on legs in the corner and Chase loved it. There was a turntable in the centre and a thick black plastic arm like death that swooped down over the shining record and *shishk*ed and *shishk*ed and *shishk*ed and then the music started like honey. Chase would squirm to get onto his back and to get his head in under the whole thing in time for the first song. He'd lie and look up into the dust-covered inner workings of the wonder and peer at the small glowing red light high up inside everything. There was only one record in the trailer, *The Clancy Brothers and Tommy Makem Live in Person at Carnegie Hall*. Chase had heard it hundreds of times. He would lie in the dark and sing along with the IRA songs, not knowing what the IRA was or where Carnegie Hall was but thinking that he would go there someday and meet the men in the big white sweaters who looked so cheerful on the cover of the record.

'Does he never get tired of those damned Republican songs?' his father asked his mother.

He never did.

&

The first real painting Chase did was of a white clapboard house by the ocean in winter with a long pale box on the porch. White and grey and pale yellow. Light blue. The horizon between the water and sky a long grey bead of paint rolling and turning blue, white and grey again.

&

There was no real tree at Christmas. Usually there were some presents Christmas morning but these would be on the kitchen table when they woke up. The tree was on the roof of the liquor store in Kemptville. It would go up on the first of December and they would usually see it a few times a week. Chase would stretch in the back seat to rest his head back and gaze up at the twinkling blue lights shining off the tinsel, the world turned upside down in the cold, the windshield blinded at the edges by the frost.

&

Trap them by getting in line and by the time you were skipping they couldn't stop you and they had to let you play then. Sometimes they pulled the rope to trip you. Sometimes not.

> *A cannibal king with a big nose ring*
> *Fell in love with a dusty maiden*
> *And every night by the pale moonlight*

Across the lake he waded
He hugged and kissed his pretty little miss
Under the bamboo tree
And every night by the pale moonlight
It sounds like this to me
mm-mwah
mm-mwah
mm-mwah de la de ladeda

Hours in the schoolyard with that when they let her play. It was naughty. The teachers didn't like it. It was about sex. Until she couldn't feel the palms of her hands from the clapping. They'd tingle all through math. When they let her play.

Can't get through life without doing for yourself. Nobody's going to do it for you, Mary thought. She loved errands, had loved errands since she was a child and had been sent to get eggs or to feed the animals or to do one of a hundred other things that needed to be done. She had never once understood the resistance in Haven and Chase over the simplest of tasks.

'Haven, go out and take down the laundry ... '

'Why?'

Why? Because we'll be naked if we don't have clothes. Because life is a series of tasks. Because they're dry. Or for God's sake, because I asked you to and because I'm your aunt and might as well be your mother and that's just the way that it is supposed to be. Haven would kick and laze about and would sometimes heed her request with resentment, but more often than not Mary would give up and do the thing herself. Maybe that was it, maybe it was her willingness to give in that had allowed Haven the freedom to avoid any effort. Mary's own mother would never have given in – but then Mary would never have thought of defying her elders. Her father, she knew, would have quickly taken a belt to that – never had, mind you, had never needed to, but would have.

She had been a dutiful daughter to her mother, she thought while she drove to the store to pick up groceries. If you'd just put away the groceries for me more than once or twice, you'd realize this is another thing to do in a continuum of things to do. Simple or complex, you just go and you do it. Roll up your sleeves. Pickle the beets. Clean the toilets.

Children did not pickle beets any longer, it seemed; she didn't think they even lowered themselves to buy pickled beets at a store. She had never seen a jar of beets in Haven's fridge. Little bottles of hot pepper sauce from Thailand, yes – she had found one of those at eight dollars a bottle in Chase's fridge once and had just put it back silently and taken out the ketchup. God knows how their toilets got cleaned. At one point, she knew, Haven had hired someone to come in and clean her toilets, which had seemed to Mary similar to paying someone to come in and change your underwear for you. She had always cleaned the toilet any time she suspected someone might drop by, just in case they passed by the bathroom and saw the porcelain less than spotless. To pay someone to come in specifically to find your toilets dirty and to clean them for you seemed – well, it seemed the type of thing you did when you had too much money, which they didn't, or when you had never learned to do the thing properly yourself, which they had, or when you had more important things to do, which they didn't. They had always had more important things to do, she thought, even when they hadn't, as if there were more important things than making your own way in the world with your own hands.

Haven had red boots. They were Giant Tiger boots but Haven didn't care. Haven knew the Giant Tiger and the Dollar Bin were different from other stores. She had just become old enough, wise enough, to know that. Old enough, wise enough, not to care. Not really.

The boots were gathering soft white flakes on their shining tops.

Falling and melting, falling and melting.

Haven thought that she was too young to die.

Chase was crying.

'Don't cry,' she told him.

He stopped.

The Apple Jacks had been one of the few things worth eating in the house so they had eaten them. She didn't know that her father was home asleep and they had not seen their mother for several days.

'I'm cold,' Chase said.

'You should have put your boots on.'

'I don't know where they are.'

Sitting cross-legged on the floor with the box of cereal when her father came around the corner from the hallway.

'We could go,' she told Chase, told herself, sitting looking at his sock feet in the snow. 'We could just go.'

'Get your goddamned hands out of my breakfast,' he'd yelled, picking up Chase and tossing him against the counter, the cupboard door splitting and rattling off its hinges.

So they went.

'And get the hell out of my house. I'll kill the both of you.'

The keys were always in the ignition, and they went.

&

This is what I think, and this is who I am, he thought. This is what I think. And this is who I am. And they're not the same thing. They're not the same. Because sometimes I'm thinking wrong. I'm thinking wrong. I don't know how to stop that.

&

It was a milk sky. Milk clouds. Not because they were white but because they were spilt, bubbling in a slant across the sky. Haven marched with a certainty through the white towards the car, pulling Chase behind her. Snow continued to drift down and Haven stood gazing up for a moment before she pulled open the driver's door. Placed her red boots on the pedals.

'Get in,' she told Chase.

'What are we doing?' he asked, pulling his wet sock feet up onto the seat.

'Leaving,' she said and she turned the key.

Haven knew how to drive from a long time ago on a day when the sun was shining and her father had let her drive the car in the field across the highway and from watching every time her father or mother drove the car, watched their feet on the pedals, their hands on the stick and wheel. She worked the clutch, mirroring what she had seen but felt like someone working a marionette for the first time and getting the strings crossed. The engine raced and the tires spun in the wet snow. She fought the wheel and got the car turned around towards the highway but felt the rear end sliding towards the ditch.

'Are we okay?' Chase asked in a small voice, too small for the high howling of the motor.

'We're going to be,' she decided.

Second gear.

They went through a mailbox, which she watched flip up over the car and land in the road in front of her father who had run from the trailer, slipping over the fresh snow and falling hard onto his side.

'Shit,' Chase said, looking out the back window at his father rolling in the snow.

'Shit,' Haven said, looking out the front at the upcoming highway and a passing truck.

'We can't go back,' she said, realizing that it was forever now. 'Hold on.'

She slowed down as much as she could and started a wide arcing turn, crossing the shoulder and sending a spray of snow and sudden gravel flying like a rainbow, slipping back onto the highway and struggling to stay on her side of the road. The engine gunning and racing.

'Slow down,' she said aloud to herself and she forced her right foot to ease slowly off the pedal.

'We're okay,' she said and drove calmly through the swerving cars and the angry horns.

'I'm turning here,' she told Chase, who had his hands braced against the dashboard.

'Okay.'

They swerved off the highway and onto a side road and from there to a concession road where she didn't have to worry about other cars.

'Where are we going to go?' Chase asked. He knew already that they could never go home now.

'Here,' Haven said, turning again onto a smaller side road, then losing all traction in the heavier snow and sliding completely off the road, slicing past trees and slipping up to the hips of the car in mud and snow, the rear wheels rendering a final high-pitched complaint as Haven's foot pressed more and more reluctantly against the pedal.

Here,' she said again and she switched off the key and rested her head against the wheel, 'we're going here.'

And they never went back.

&

One time Chase had walked into the Bright Star after being awake for a few days, his eyes red-rimmed and unfocused, his clothes rumpled and uneven.

'What happened to you?' the waitress asked, pouring him a coffee.

'How far back do you want to go?' he asked her, and then, 'What kind of pie do you have?'

&

Day shift. Night shift. They cleaned. The summer Haven was five, her mother got a job at the motel. She went in during the day when the guests were out and cleaned the rooms. At night she did the laundry. Worked in the office. It wasn't that far from where they lived, but on the days her father took the car they had to walk and it took a long time. Chase kicked at the gravel and looked for cans in the ditch. Haven remembered her feet being sore by the time they got there. Her shoes got scuffed. They were black and shiny and she tried to keep them that way but they kept getting scratches on them and soon they weren't like little mirrors on her feet anymore. There was no way to protect them.

Sometimes her mother took her hand when they were walking by the highway and trucks passed. Sometimes she didn't. Her mother had a brown uniform that she wore when she went

118

to work. One time a big truck stopped and she remembered her mother talking to the driver and the driver saying something, she didn't understand what, and then her mother saying, 'Fuck you,' and grabbing her hand and Chase's hand and turning and walking away, pulling them along.

Haven's job at the motel was to collect any ashtrays and take them out behind building and empty them into a big pile of ashes by some trees and then collect all the ashtrays together and take them to the little room where the mops and things were stored and wash them out in a big dirty sink with a rag. There was a big dirty mirror over the sink and she made faces in it. The clearest part of the memory was the big pile of ashes just at the edge of the woods behind the motel. All summer it just kept getting bigger until it rained and then it shrunk down a bit. And washing them in the big sink. The ashes and the water went together to make a paste.

She remembered that her mother packed two digestive cookies into an old cough-drop tin each morning and when it was time to take a break she and Chase would sit out by the trees and have the cookies or sometimes when the manager wasn't around they could sit in the room her mother was cleaning and watch TV. She liked *Sesame Street* and in some of the rooms there was cable and she could watch *Captain Kangaroo*. The digestive cookies were just the perfect round size to fit in the cough-drop tin. It was like it had been made to carry digestive cookies. It was like a coffin for digestive cookies. There were cherries painted on the lid of the tin. They were raised in the metal like little bumps. You could feel them with your finger.

She never thought about it until years later, that there was never a sandwich. Never a drink.

The mothers on TV made big dinners sometimes and served them on tablecloths. Sometimes her mother made big dinners too and they all sat down together and ate at the table in the kitchen. They'd have chicken. Or meatloaf. Sometimes. And they'd have dessert too, McCain cake. In one of those shows there was a housekeeper who lived in the house with the family in her own room and she had a uniform the same as her mother's.

Paint is to a brush as mustard is to a _____.

That was a question on a test she took in high school. It was to measure intelligence to see what you could do after high school.

Haven looked at the question and thought:

My mother is to other mothers as plywood is to oak.

She didn't know what made her think that. Then she couldn't stop thinking that and then she couldn't finish the test. But they let her take it another day and that's when they told Mary that Haven could take whatever she wanted in university. That she'd be able to handle it. So she had ended up in pre-med, Mary working two jobs and applying for grants and loans. Then they thought forensics would be a good focus for her. She could help people end their grief. She could find answers for them. But they hadn't thought about the pictures of injured children. They hadn't considered those.

As plywood is to oak. Kind of the same, but not quite as strong. Made up of all kinds of things. Pressed together. Good for some jobs. Not for others. Not strong enough.

A knife.

Paint is to a brush as mustard is to a knife. She got it right the second time.

Because she wasn't thinking about her mother. Which always made things easier.

&

Going to take hours to copy these notes. Should have just gone to class.

> subject remains found in dumpster fire
> possibly child – small adult
> possibly female – pelvic structure
> orientation of body
> severe distortion to body cavities and planes
> autopsy shows evidence in airway tissues of
>   carboxyhaemoglobin
> evidence of swallowing of burnt debris
> soot deposition in esophagus and stomach,
>   trachea and main bronchi
> suggesting subject alive when fire started
> removal of jaw for any possible dental identification
> toxicological specimens for carbon monoxide, cyanide
> X-ray results
> bullet track from one side of brain to other, fragments
>   in skull anterior
> facial bones show possible beating
> forensic ordontologist required

She turned the page. Looked at the pictures. Felt it on her for days.

That had been close to the end. Just couldn't do that anymore. It wasn't worth all that it cost her.

It wasn't bad to be different. It didn't mean he was bad. It was a hot buzzing in his skull, a warm electrical syrup that poured down the back of his neck and drove him into the ground, staring without seeing, the air thick like a flock of heavy birds around his head. It was usually in the forest. It was when he went to the forest. He held his breath until the air stood still about him. He knew he was different. This didn't happen to other people. They'd talk about it. He'd know. And the way he talked to himself. All the time. Had to do it. Had to. Had to. The way he talked. Couldn't stop.

&

Chase steered the car with care around the leg of the bed and into the shade under the quilt. His father and his mother were going away. Got his head right down to the floor to see what it would look like through the window of the car: a sea of carpet and a looming night table. Going away. Which was a long way. But then they would be back. After that maybe they would be back. Maybe not, though. There was a chance maybe not. Nobody knew. Aunt Mary said his mom might fight to get them back. Chase pictured her in a boxing ring having to fight someone.

'It's too late for her,' he heard Aunt Mary say on the phone.

Pictured his mother alone in the ring. No other fighter showing up.

'She'll be able to see them, not to have them, not while I'm here.'

Steered his parents around a large yellow robot lying on the carpet. Drove the car under the bed and left it there. Maybe not.

&

'You always look at me like I want it to be this way, like this is the way that I planned it. Nobody wants things to be like this – you think I want it like this?'

His father was sitting at the kitchen table with his beer and explaining things to Chase.

'You've got to be strong,' his father told him. 'World's gonna fuckin' eat you up, boy.'

Chase didn't say anything. It was better to be quiet.

'Spit you out … '

Chase didn't say anything.

'You're not ready … '

&

Never been in a house like it, either of them. The house they had moved to with Aunt Mary wasn't a new house but it was new to them. And it wasn't the house in Haven's head, but it was closer to it than the trailer had ever been. Aunt Mary said it was the best she could afford.

'It's solid,' she decided for them and they moved in. 'You two need something solid.'

It had once been a farmhouse and sat on a little hill over-looking all of the land that had once been its own and that now held, tightly packed, the houses and the strip mall that had taken the place of its corn stalks and cows.

Haven and Chase wandered through the rooms pulling at loose wallpaper and shaky doorknobs.

'We'll fix it up,' Mary told them, 'you'll see.'

They didn't have to see. It was like the idea of home that they had carried in their heads. It was real.

&

Chase always had to talk Aunt Mary into going to the art gallery. She put up a fight but he knew she'd break down in the end every time.

123

'What'll you give me?' she asked.

'I'll do the dishes for a week,' he told her.

'And the laundry,' Aunt Mary said.

'And the laundry,' he agreed.

'And put the laundry away and – '

Chase waited.

' – rub my feet.'

'Okay,' he said.

She raised an eyebrow.

'Okay,' he said again.

Chase liked the gallery for the paintings. Aunt Mary liked it for the soup and the crackers. Each time they went they would end up in the cafeteria on the top floor. Aunt Mary would crumble up her crackers while they were still in the cellophane package and then dump them in her bowl.

'Like in Paris,' she said, stirring them around.

And you could see way out over the canal and the bridges and Chase figured it probably was what Paris was like.

Eventually they were going every couple of weeks. Haven went there to see her mother. There was a painting on the fifth floor where the old paintings hung in heavy gold frames and in one there was a crowd of people in the square of a city that looked like Italy and there was a face in that crowd that looked like what she remembered of her mother. In front of the gold dome of a huge church. While Chase and Aunt Mary wandered through the Group of Seven, Haven would make the excuse of going to the washroom or finding a water fountain and she would glide smoothly to the fifth floor on the elevator and sit before her painting on a low bench with leather cushions that let air out of themselves slowly when you sat on them and each had a little button sewn at the centre. Haven would sit until they would come and find her. People would walk right in front of her sometimes as if

124

she wasn't there and she would crane her neck around them to see her mother's face craning back through the crowd in the piazza. She found the word in a book from the school library about Italian paintings. Like *pizza* with an *ahhh*. *Piaahhzza*. I'll meet you in the *piaahhzzah*. Just in front of the gold dome.

Near where my mother stands. Waiting.

Where I sit with the guard watching and a pool of light and the air conditioner humming.

The paint was old and glossed over but if you got up close you could see tiny cracks that were no wider than eyelashes in the yellow of her mother's face. The first couple of visits the security guards got fidgety when she got up close but after a while they got used to her. Most of the time she would just sit on the bench anyway and look from there. The tiny cracks in the paint no wider than eyelashes.

In the *piaahhzzaah*.

&

'How much to fix it?'

The mechanic stood looking at the Jeep. 'There's only so much that can be fixed,' he said.

Chase nodded.

&

It is a scientific fact that no two snowflakes are the same. Snowflakes grow with a perfect six-sided symmetry. Water molecules crystallize around a microscopic speck of dust. The snowflake expands by adding billions and billions of water molecules around the edges. The basic six-fold symmetry of the crystal is due to the shape of the water molecules, which link to form hexagons. But what tells the molecules attaching at one point of the snowflake how the molecules are doing on another point, a billion molecules away? How is the detailed overall symmetry maintained? No amount of scientific investigation has ever solved this puzzle.

It all seemed pointless then, if scientists had tried for years to come up with an answer and had failed. It was then, at seventeen, standing in the high school library, that she decided to become a scientist, a doctor, to know things – seduced by pointlessness and by six-sided symmetry.

Not enough experience to practice on live patients yet. And the dead ones didn't provide much opportunity to develop a bedside manner. So there were student volunteers from other faculties and older medical students who were trained to be mock patients for the first-year students, the baby docs. Haven was assigned a routine physical examination of a middle-aged woman with the improbable name of Mrs. Flo Mooney. Martin, the session instructor, explained that Mrs. Mooney was in radio marketing and had two children, no record of serious health concerns. Her file showed a broken leg three years ago (skiing) and some bursitis (tennis). Nothing out of the ordinary. Haven had seen the woman around campus, in the library, she thought. She was the type of woman who wore caftans. Whatever type that was – the caftan type. She looked like a prof from the English Department. She drank herbal teas and had a group of girlfriends with whom she met regularly at this café or that restaurant. They discussed the books they'd read or the men they'd slept with. Haven wiped her mind like a chalkboard. Stop. Focus. Nervous.

Stop.

'How are you feeling today?' she asked.

'Don't lead with symptoms – ask her about the weather,' Martin broke in. 'She may be here to see you for something she's very nervous about. You'd be surprised how many patients are already convinced that they have cancer. Change tack.'

Haven looked back to the patient, who smiled encouragingly. Haven drew a blank.

'The weather,' Martin prompted.

'Right. Is it still raining, Mrs. Mooney?'

After that it went smoothly. Haven took her blood pressure and listened to her chest. She suggested a mammogram based on age and family history. She imagined going home and watching cooking shows or doing her laundry. Mrs. Mooney was buttoning up her blouse.

'Good,' Martin said, 'good.'

The next week Martin and the group reviewed Haven's examination of Mrs. Mooney and the pretend mammography results, which lay before them on a smooth white table. A spot on the right breast.

'Right,' Martin began. 'Good news or bad news first?'

There was a pause.

'What's the good news?' Haven asked.

Martin shrugged. 'Make some up?' he suggested.

No one spoke.

'You'll have to,' he added, pointing to the sheet. ''Cause that shit's well into her lymph nodes and it's gonna kill her. Look, what's important is that she gets the news and that the news itself doesn't kill her. The cancer – if it is cancer, it'll have to be biopsied – it'll kill her eventually, but the news definitely should not.'

Martin waited for someone to speak.

'What's the right answer? What's the right way to do it?' someone asked.

Martin shrugged again. 'There isn't one,' he said. 'Whatever way gets the news to her without killing her and gets her out of your office and home to her family in as few pieces as possible. Anyway, it doesn't have to be cancer, might not be. She has to wait for a biopsy, emphasize that – leave her something to hope for, leave her with some control.'

Haven waited a moment.

'Is it cancer?' she asked.

'Of course.'

'The results of your mammogram show that there's a shadow on your right breast that's larger than it should be.'

'What?'

Haven went blank.

'What does that mean?'

'I'm sorry … '

Mrs. Mooney feigned terror. 'My mother died of cancer!'

'I'm sorry … ' Haven looked down at the table.

'Haven … ' Martin prompted.

'I'm sorry.'

Haven looked up and out the window. Heard herself speaking.

'I'm sorry, but I can't help you.'

And then it came out.

'You're going to die.'

It ended it how it began: with a whimper.

'There are dark and hidden magical things inside me, girl,' Ken had told her.

But there weren't.

'I'm deep.'

And he wasn't.

His lips were always dry.

Chase would tuck himself down in the seat as his father drove drunkenly through snowstorms and sun, beaches, birthday parties and Scout meetings. Many people had done it then, but his father had done it all the time, always a bottle somewhere, always a glass. Sounds of clinking under the car seats. Dark rings of moisture left on everything. His Scoutmaster talking to his father after the Ford had dinged another car in the gravel parking lot behind the church, Chase standing short in the sun. It was a debate between two belt buckles, one loose and hanging, one brightly polished, in which he could see himself reflected as the man said, 'I think your father needs one or two fewer drinks in the middle of the day.'

And even then Chase knew it was wrong – for his father to be drunk, yes, but for one man to speak of another man like that to his son – and the next week he quit the Scouts. Just left.

Pretty much the biggest thing he'd ever seen. It was bigger than he thought a bear could be. Not that it mattered either way. A bear was a bear.

&

The sleeves were too long. Chase never felt comfortable in his own clothes and was always pulling at them. Shirts too tight, pants too short, collars choking at him. Never felt comfortable naked either. Looked at his face in the mirror and saw someone else. He didn't know what to do.

&

'How beautiful,' Mary said just before she died.

It was the first time she had spoken in several months.

'How beautiful … '

Haven held her hand. A sponge to her mouth. Dry skin spots. Warm going cold. Slipping.

&

It was mid-afternoon. How do people do it, Chase wondered. He swirled the bottom of his beer in the well of the glass and watched the wave of yellow and white circle around. How do people get through mid-afternoon? It was the hardest time of the day. Sometimes it was worse than the middle of the night. Let his mind be random. Random. In that. Thinking of nothing. Nothing in that. How do people get through the mid-afternoon with its quiet and its refusal to be morning or evening or even late afternoon and its waning light in April and its clouds that hang over the street and pass and continue? Its waning light in April and its clouds that hang. He ordered another beer. Clouds that hang. One way to get by it. He liked the little glasses they served with the beer. A bottle of beer and the little glass next to it, pitted and marked from the dishwasher. He knew from having worked there how quickly the glasses were aged by the heat of the water and by the detergent. Had to keep buying new glasses because they bought cheap ones. They didn't know anything about glasses, they knew about Chinese food, how to make good Chinese food. They didn't know about glasses. Liked the way the glass sat next to the bottle and it was small enough you could pour it out three times and feel like you were getting somewhere. Looked at the cars in the grey light. Still too cold to be spring yet. The window streaked and pitted like the glass. Couldn't count the ways.

Heard it like someone crinkling up cellophane wrap and then saw the rain hit the street. Somebody running to get inside. Water drumming the window. Only took a minute for rivers to start running down the gutters. Cars slowing down and then it stopped. Stopped. Stopped. And the clouds passing. How did people do it?

To the back pew. As soon as he got in. Wherever Haven was sitting he was still going to sit at the back. He even parked at the back of the church instead of the front where all the other cars were. He wasn't drunk, just drinking. If he was drunk Haven would know. She would be able to tell. His suit was sticky. He popped a Mento into his mouth. It was July and a heavy heat had descended. Haven had chosen to have the funeral at Resurrection of Our Lord parish since Mary had attended there more than anywhere else. That's what Haven had said. *Resurrection of Our Lord. Be there on time, Chase.*

He hadn't been sure he was going until he was almost there. He had managed to put it from his mind almost up to the point where the front fender of his Jeep nudged into the rear of the car parked in front of it. The sun was burning the sky and grass and preventing him from seeing clearly out the windshield. He squinted and held up a hand to the light to stare at the building tucked into the tightly bungalowed street. Chase emptied his bottle and looked around for a place to put it, finally tossing into a nearby dumpster.

Inside he edged to the side of the vestibule and attempted to disappear into the bulletin board advertising babysitting courses and Bible study groups.

A silver-haired man sidled up to him. 'There are seats up in the front,' he whispered mintily.

'That's all right,' Chase answered.

'We're all family here,' the man answered, lightly brushing his lapel to draw attention, Chase thought, to a pin that identified him as an usher.

'No. It's all right … ' Chase attempted to shrink back further into the cork and the thumbtacks.

'You're sure? The front pew is open.'

The man continued in a hushed tone and then shrugged slightly as if to suggest that it was now between Chase and his God as to why he chose to stay hidden back here rather than to go up front where the real Christians were. Chase studied a notice about Sunday school and a sign-up sheet for refreshments: cookies and brownies, little sandwiches. Chase moved slightly further along the wall nearer the corner of the room. What was the room exactly, he wondered, a vestibule? A nave? A sacristy? He fidgeted with his tie and looked down at his hands. Felt as if he were standing in a closet.

When he had first stolen a glance into the church towards the altar, he had seen both the open casket and a framed portrait sitting atop the burnished oak. A silver-haired lady smiling. Chase had quickly looked away, feeling threatened by too great a degree of detail. He had not been working June or July and he knew that during that time he must have been doing something but he now had no idea what, could not remember more than a few things. He remembered stopping the Jeep by the side of the road shortly after Haven called to tell him, carefully placing his forehead on the edge of the steering wheel and stealing great shuddering and silent sobs of breath as if he were being repeatedly pushed and held under water and let up only for quick snatches of air. He remembered saying out loud, to someone – to who? – that he could not take this, that he was tired. Really tired. That this was too much.

The sounds of greeting began from within the church and Chase shifted his gaze. He stood and listened to the progression of the ceremony as it unfolded in muted tones and music. The doors to the outside opened and an older woman entered and exchanged a pleasant smile of recognition with a man to Chase's right, as if they were meeting on an elevator or at a salad bar. He hadn't recognized anyone so far and wondered how all these people knew Mary and why he hadn't ever met any of them. If these people could gather together here as if nothing were really wrong, then perhaps he could convince himself of it too. That the woman lying quietly in the next room had completed all of her trips to the grocery store and her cooking, had finished up her last cup of tea, gradually lost all of her memory, faded away slowly to an infant again, moved into the home and without event passed away of natural causes.

He supposed Haven must be right up front. If he had been here earlier, she would have found him and brought him there. He would have preferred to be at the back but he wanted her to know he was there. She would be mad if she thought he hadn't come and that would spoil the ceremony for her. Could you spoil a funeral like you could a party or a wedding? Probably. Leave it to him. He edged closer to the doorway, smiling apologies, but could not find the back of her head. Maybe there on the right?

As the service continued, Chase found that it became easier and easier to imagine himself a part of this group of people and he began to feel less of a spy and then he realized that the priest had begun to speak of Mary and provide details of her life, a life that had apparently been rather wonderful. There were things Chase had not known. Why hadn't Haven told him? The priest's voice was raised now and tremulous as he described Mary's love of and way with flowers and with small children. It was hard to hear everything from where he was.

'We know she loved them, you could see that she loved them, loved them all.'

Chase tried to think of any small children that Mary had been close to besides Haven and him.

'I'm going to get carried away here,' he told the congregation, 'and you know how I get carried away in the Lord … '

Several people inside nodded and the man across the foyer from Chase smiled and nodded.

He spoke then of how Mary had always gathered children, her own and others, around her, and hadn't she been driving to pick up children when this tragedy had befallen her, but don't for a second let ourselves think that this is a tragedy, he said, *tragedy* is our word and not the Lord's, not the Lord's …

Mary had been in the home for months. Chase had visited her there. She had Alzheimer's. She couldn't remember what day it was, let alone how to drive a car. She shouldn't have been driving a car.

'She has simply gone home. And we are sad only in that she has seen fit to leave us behind, that the Lord has seen fit to wait a little longer for the rest of us.'

For the rest of us, Chase thought, and he nodded his head. He became very aware of the heat and wondered how people were standing it. His head felt tight and his tongue large, little balls of sweat dropping from his armpits.

'But the choir in heaven must have been short one voice, and that voice must surely be a voice we all remember in this very church, in this very choir.'

Chase didn't remember Mary having ever been in a choir. *Shut your gaping hole*, he remembered her yelling up the stairs when Haven practiced her choir songs at home. *Just 'cause God's in His heaven doesn't mean you have to sing that loud for Christ's sake, He'll still hear you.*

'You could do worse,' the priest continued, 'than to spend the rest of your life, the whole thing, just listening for that voice again, because that voice would now be a voice from heaven.'

Chase's head nodded again.

'I go to prepare a place for you, that's what our Savior said … and you know that He had a place prepared for our Elizabeth Rose, what a wonderful place.'

Well, that was it then, Chase thought sadly. He was at the wrong funeral. He had got it wrong somehow, got the day wrong or the time, got things wrong again.

He was aware that tears were streaming down his face only when the woman next to her reached over and squeezed his forearm firmly. What a very nice thing to have done, Chase thought, an almost covert thing the way that they were standing there by the notice board, placed tightly together. What a very nice thing to do. Sincere. And then he felt sick, felt as if he would throw up and that he must get away and he almost fell through the glass doors, pushing hard on the metal bar to open it and then falling, spinning almost blindly onto the sunlit grass, which came quickly up to meet him and it had been then, as the woman followed him and put her arms around him there on the lawn and asked, 'Are you all right?'

That Chase knew for certain that he was not. No, he was not. He was not.

&

Be pretty sad if God had to wonder if He was real. God didn't think about whether or not God existed. He didn't have to. That thought wouldn't enter His mind like it did Chase's. That's because he was a sinner. A sinner.

&

Where is he, Haven wondered. He'd better get here soon. April kept turning and looking around the church. Haven tapped her on the leg and brought both her hands to her lap, palms down. Settle yourself. There are no boys at the funeral, she wanted to say. That was a horrible thing to think. Maybe she was just looking for Chase. Who should be here by now.

April tugged at the short sleeves of her blouse. She had a short black skirt, a white blouse and a trim black jacket she had taken off just before sitting and laid neatly across the back of the pew. Like a grown-up, Haven thought. They'd had to buy everything. Haven thought the clothes made April move more slowly. Put an end to the dervish that usually occupied her. Haven had told her the blouse made her look like Jacqueline Kennedy and then realized April probably didn't know who that was and didn't feel like explaining it so just told her that it was a compliment and let it go. April kept looking back to check the door. She was looking for Chase. She had a thin silver necklace with a locket that she wore over her blouse. There was nothing in the locket. Nobody knew that. She looked so quiet and respectful. A church girl.

There's more to growing up, April, Haven remembered Mary saying, *than acting like a bitch all the time.*

Haven looked up. That was Mrs. Conway who just sat down. She used to visit Mary and the two of them would sit close together at the table talking and they would cook thick syrupy tea in a little kettle on the stove. Haven caught her eye and smiled at her in a way that she knew a friend of Mary's would like, a church way, she thought, like a church girl. Quiet and shy and respectful. Why wasn't she crying? There was something wrong with her that she wasn't crying at her own aunt's funeral. April wasn't crying either. She sat with her head tilted down – was she praying? She had cried last night and Haven had cried with her. It was all right not to be crying, she had already cried, and then suddenly she was crying again and she put her arm around April who did not try to pull away.

Haven saw Mrs. Conway looking over at them and she bowed her head like April, like she was praying.

How much laundry could the three of them possibly make? There were times when the anger just came out in all directions. Haven recalled feeling perfectly justified throwing clothespin after clothespin onto the line, virtually stapling the clothes onto the rope, and happily imagining Aunt Mary's fury when she came out with the basket ready to collect the clothes for a rapid and machine-like sorting.

Most of all she remembered the weathered tree branch that was used to prop up the line in the middle when it sagged with the weight of the wet clothes. It had been the same stick for as long as Haven could remember, Aunt Mary having pulled it off a tree for that purpose years earlier and notched it at one end to fit the line, and the years of damp weight had worn the groove deeper and deeper, and when she angled the stick and caught up the line it had been like a sail catching the wind.

&

On Mary's advice, Haven began praying to the Virgin Mary at the age of twenty-eight.

'Don't waste your time on the others,' Mary said. 'She's one of us.'

'What, Irish? She wasn't Irish, Mary.'

'May as well have been. A poor woman – she was a woman, is what I mean, she was one of us. She understands what women go through in this world, and also Catholics are the only ones allowed to pray to her – it's like a direct line.' She dumped the onions into a pot on the stove. 'So don't be so proud.'

'I'm not so proud.'

'Anyone – pass me those tomatoes – anyone who makes cardboard signs as a teenager and stands in the road trying to hitchhike a ride away from her family carries a certain amount of misplaced pride. Just talk to her, that's all I'm saying ... talk ...'

So Haven did.

&

As real a thing as Chase had ever seen. First it was a shape in his mind. It was a shifting in the trees and a sound. Then it was real. It was the realest thing ever.

&

Good Copy Report Transcript.
File 16288-07.

Office of the Coroner
Post-Mortem Examination Report

Date Received: September 20, 1700 hours

General Information
A 37-year-old white male reportedly attacked and mauled by a black bear. Subject was pronounced dead at the scene.

The deceased is received in a white sheet, clothed in blue denim trousers, cotton briefs, a cotton lumberjack shirt and blue socks.

Multiple facial fractures, multiple lacerations and a fractured femur.

General Description
Rigor mortis is generalized and full. The corneas are markedly opaque and the body is cool to the touch.

The body is well-developed and well-nourished. Upper extremities free from injuries. The scalp hair is dark and exhibits a large amount of red-brown clotted blood. The head is symmetrical and displays several abrasions, contusions and lacerations. An older scar lies recedent from the hairline.

Evidence of Injury
Blunt-force injuries of the head:
    Severe lacerations to head, neck, shoulders and chest.
    The scalp is reflected revealing sub-galeal contusions.

Blunt-force injuries of the neck:

A layer-by-layer dissection of the neck performed. The larynx and hyoid bone are intact. The cervical spine displays evidence of hemorrhage into the surrounding tissues. Fractures of the second and third sub-cervical vertebrae with associated incomplete dissection of the spinal cord.

A 1-inch contusion was present on the back of the forearm. Situated over the right upper back were two diagonally oriented interrupted abrasions, each measuring about 4 1/2 inches. They were interspaced by a distance of 1/2 inch. Situated below this abrasion and on the left side was a 4 by 2 inch area of contusion. Below this contusion, extending to the right mid back, were two linear diagonally oriented abrasions interspaced by a distance of 2/16 inch.

Situated over the right gluteal were multiple linear scratches measuring from 1/2 inch to 3/8 inch. Punctate linear scratches were present on the inferior aspect of the left buttocks region.

Evidence of Therapeutic Intervention
None.

Summary of Autopsy Findings
Blunt-force injuries: Head. Scalp contusions with associated sub-galeal hemorrhage in the right temporal region.

Subject experienced massive shock and trauma and asphyxiated on own blood due to massive laceration to neck with complications due to severing of spinal cord which was incomplete but decisive.

The summer she was sixteen, Haven thought, it had all seemed to make a sort of sense. She had been in love with a boy named Bib. He hadn't known who she was, they never spoke. But that summer he looked at her once at the pool in the park where they went for lessons and she was certain that the world was starting. He never looked at her again, but the charge of that moment hung with her and informed the declining winter months that followed. That look and the feel of the sun baking the concrete, the warmth of the grey wire fence that burned your skin when you touched it, the light off the chlorine water. The cries of the kids on the hot metal slide. The world starting. And Bib, whom she could not remember ever having seen again.

There was the time he felt clear. Saw everything the way that it really was. He thought. Once.

'People waste a lot of time,' Chase said, turning to look at Mary across the counter in the kitchen.

'Yes, they do,' she agreed.

And they had a cup of tea together. Listened to the sound of the geese flying close over the roof of the house in the rain and the softly echoed sounds of Haven's radio upstairs.

So let's see what the dictionary says about it, Haven thought. There were thirty definitions for the letter D. Just for the letter. She flipped through the pages.

And then she stopped and looked at the top entry on the open page:

> *daughter*
> *One's female child.*
> *A female descendant.*
> *A woman considered as if in relationship of child to parent.*
> *One personified or regarded as a female descendant.*
> *Possessing the characteristics of a daughter.*

Now she was at the point of looking at the word and not being able to see it. Was that really how you spelled *daughter*? It didn't look right.

> *Daughter.*
> *Daughter.*
> *Daughter.*
> *Daughter.*
> *Daughter.*

Daughter. She said it over until it sounded strange in her head. *Daughter.*

> *Daughterly.*
> *Day.*
> *The period of light between dawn and nightfall.*
> *The interval between sunrise and sunset.*

As if that's all that it was.

Chase did not eat bacon. Or ham. Or sausage.

Because of the pig. Because of the pig roast and how it had begun, which was slowly and without clear indication of direction. His father told him to get ready, that they were going to a barbecue. His father had been drinking a lot of beer. His father was playing the bad man. That's what Haven called it when you couldn't tell what he was going to do but you knew it wouldn't be any good. *Playing the bad man.* Chase didn't know what it meant to get ready for a barbecue, so he put on his shoes and waited by the door.

'Are we all going?' Haven asked.

'No.'

Haven looked towards Chase and shrugged. Raised her hands. 'Why not?'

Chase held his breath. His father said nothing. *There's nothing I can do,* Haven told him with her eyes.

'C'mon,' his father said, 'we're going.'

So they went, across the patchwork of gravel roads that crossed back and forth behind the trailer park. Chase pressed his forehead against the window and counted the mailboxes. He and Haven counted mailboxes to keep track of how far from home they were. How far the drive home would be if everyone was drunk. If the car was weaving from one side of the road to the other.

Fifteen.

Twenty-eight.

Thirty-four.

His father always had a beer first. After that it might be anything but it would always be a lot and it would always take a long time. He had never seen these people before but his father knew all of them and they seemed happy to see him. Most of them seemed to be pretty drunk already and some of them looked at him and smiled, and a man said, 'Hey,' and rubbed the top of his head.

Once at school, after the field trip to the museum, kids had been talking about the slanted kitchen.

'It was crazy,' one said.

'Yeah, it was like being drunk,' Chase had said, laughing along.

Everyone stopped and looked at him.

His father told him to come along around to a big barn where they were getting dinner ready. You could hear the pig squealing from all over the place – he had heard it as they pulled into the driveway, but as they came around the barn there was suddenly a pig attached to the sound. Three men were wrestling with the pig and trying to lift it onto a large wooden table. The pig was putting up a huge fight. One man had its front legs and another its rear, and the third man seemed to be holding the table as if it might try to run as well. They were dancing through empty bottles and swearing and inching their way in a shuffle towards the table when the man in the rear went down and let go of the pig, leaving the man in the front to slide slowly down into the dirt with the bucking, screaming pig trying to climb up his body as if it were escaping from quicksand. The third man jumped over the table and threw himself down on the back of the pig. Chase could tell that the struggle was shifting and that the pig was getting the upper hand. If the pig managed to get away he'd be gone for a while.

'Stick 'im now,' shouted one of the men, and the man who was still rolling in the dirt suddenly had a long knife and was standing and steadying it close to the pig's throat.

'Hold him,' he said.

'What the hell do you think we're doing?'

The first man was trying to keep the pig's head back in a choke hold. The pig had seen the knife and the squealing had entered a whole new volume of desperation and panic. Chase couldn't believe that what was going to happen was going to happen. And then it did. The man drove the knife into the centre of the pig's throat at the bottom and seemed to wrestle with it as if it were stuck there. The cries of the pig became purple in the air and blood started to spray out of its mouth and spill in regular pulses out of the new hole in its throat that bloomed wider and wider. Chase thought that maybe he would throw up or go weak in the knees and fall but he stayed where he was, shaking a little in his fingers, his eyes fixed on the strange widening hole that shouldn't be there and on the three men who rolled in the reddening dirt. Together they managed to heave the wildly protesting animal onto the table finally and the man with the knife continued his work until there was silence. Chase looked up at his father who would not look down at him but who calmly and deliberately took a pack of cigarettes from his pocket and struck a match with one steady hand.

&

'You'll be here just for a short time until we have a home for you,' Carol was saying.

Carol was always in a blouse and a crisp skirt. She smelled like mints.

'Which should be by the end of the week, only a few days.'

She was writing something on some papers at a counter. Haven and Chase stood by her looking around. There were some people sitting in chairs. Carol had a badge with her picture on it clipped to her skirt. It looked like the people were waiting to go into some of the rooms for meetings. There was a man with a briefcase who smiled at Haven. The doors had little signs with people's names. The phone kept ringing.

What she'd done was so big.

It had ended, finally, with Ivy. Mostly because he couldn't imagine it going on. He sat one afternoon looking at the drapes of light across her long legs on the bed, waiting for her to wake up and give the light some purpose by moving her legs beneath it. Her skin the reason for the light being there. Knowing that when she woke he would break his own heart with what he would say to her. How the words would feel too large in his mouth. How his throat would close up on them.

'Ivy, I … '

Her skin, warm. Eyes open.

'What is it?'

For weeks after they were taken from their parents – after they were never returned to their parents, after they had been taken from the car in the frozen marsh – nobody had told them anything. Then they found out that the police had found seven guns in the trailer. Five rifles under the bed, two handguns in the dresser, even a handgun in the trunk of the car they got away in. Hidden inside the spare tire. Seven guns. What had he been thinking? What had he been protecting himself against? She remembered the way the Children's Aid lady had told her. Behind the concern there had been an enjoyment, like she had been watching Haven through glass. Do you know what your father did? Did you know what your father had?

So she tried to think in his favour. Seven guns and never used one, she thought. That's something.

And the hell with you, she thought.

&

Right to the bottom, he could tell. The size of it. The shape of it. The way it would feel in his hands. Rough. Like this. Eventually it would take him down. He'd carried everything down from the Jeep to the canoe. He would just sink down. It would be like that. It would be okay. The concrete was cold and the yellow rope scratched his hands. Should have got the soft white rope. It had been more expensive, which was stupid to think of. It had been soft in his hands at the store. Like a rabbit. He should have got the white rope. He thought he should have a lock or something so he couldn't change his mind and untie everything. He wouldn't do that. Wouldn't wouldn't wouldn't do that. It was the way that it should be. Then he wouldn't have to worry. Anymore. Things wouldn't always be edging around him like they were pointing at him. Get things out of his head. This thing and that thing every time he opened his eyes or thought of something or thought of something else. Every time. A machine that wouldn't stop.

and Haven

and Haven

All that. And Haven would be fine. He wouldn't be leaving her. Wouldn't do that. Not really. He unzipped the tent and looked out. It was cold again. His Oh Henry! wrappers were spread out between the trees. His empty can of beans and the newspaper he had used to clean the pot in the dark. Something had torn the bag down from the tree and spread it around in the dark. Raccoons. He'd tie Lucky to the tree so the rangers would find him. Haven would want Lucky safe. Want him back. They'd find him soon enough. They came around each day. He'd leave him a dish of water.

He dragged the concrete blocks and rope down to the canoe.

The lake a silver sheet.

Lucky barking.

&

Live. Die. Only.
Onlyonlyonlyonlyonlyonlyonlyonlyonlyonlyonlyonlyonly
onlyonlyonlyonlyonlyonlyonlyonlyonlyonlyonlyonly
onlyonlyonlyonlyonlyonlyonlystop
onlystop
only think about this: hands on the rough concrete and the too-
yellow rope
only stop
smell of pine and the little waves on the bottom of the canoe
tapping
pine smelled clean
they made cleaners that smelled like pine so you'd think of clean
tie the rope tight under your arms around your chest like this
or around your neck safer
nobody around
look
no, nobody
sound of a splash far off
fish, a rock, a beaver
sit and think and look out over the water
knees cold against the fibreglass
look out over the water
last look
cold
my sleeves are frayed
lumberjack shirt
water far down silver blue green then black
finish black final end
touch cold
quiet

deep
sleep
there
wet
warm in the bed
my sleeves are frayed
torn at the edges
blocks hold over the water
okay
run the rope through
like this
hands burning
then cold down
pulling
pulling

Haven could fix those, though.
Haven could fix those sleeves with her sewing.
Give them to Haven.
Pull up the blocks and give your shirt to Haven.
And not leave her alone.
Not alone.
Ever.

he was walking back to the tent before he saw it and then the
thought was in front of him and it wasn't raccoons it wasn't
raccoons it was a bear cub look at that and then it was a bear and
it was the mother bear and he couldn't make it to the tent and
Lucky was barking and he couldn't make it back to the canoe what
are you supposed to do supposed to fall down lie on the ground

like you're dead like you're already dead don't get up it's coming closer pulled closer lumberjack shirt so big and breathing breathing breath like dirt and plants hot at my neck and pressing on my back and what's it going to do what's it going to do pulling my shirt I'm moving it's clawing going to going to have to get up and run run pulling me roaring pulling me and pushing down angry it's angry at me those are claws through my shirt claws in my back in my back can't get up pushing on me if I could just I can't get my legs to move in the dirt I can't get up I can't I can't I can't I can't I can't I can't I can't I can't I can't I can't I can't breathe those are its teeth those are its teeth those are its teeth it's turning me over and Lucky barking and Lucky barking

   there's a hole in the sky
   so big
   those are its teeth
   those are

Three

The things that took place at night,
under the cover of darkness.

The pictures of it were like pornography. She flipped through them in the library. The stacks you could get to only if you were in med. Had to show your card. It was closing in ten minutes. She needed to have this assignment done. Examples of the violence done to bodies. To people. One body had rope burns around and around it and cigarette burns. One body had been torn apart. One body. Somebody. She dropped the course. It was a compulsory course. She dropped out.

❧

'You're goin' to bed, all right, you're goin' to bed right the fuck now, you're either goin' to bed right now or you're goin' in a fuckin' coffin.'

❧

So this is the deal. The deal. The deal. This is the deal. He could park on the crossing. Right on the tracks. He didn't want to stand there. He didn't want to get out of the Jeep and stand there. Didn't want to do that. Little stones crunching under his feet. No. He opened another little bottle of Cutty and drained it. But he could do that. He could park the Jeep there. Not to stay. Just to be there. Stay long enough. Just long enough. And then go. Home.

He put it into first and drove forward. Stopped. Nothing coming. Looked both ways. Nothing coming. The Jeep's engine shuddered. It did that. Nothing. Well. He opened another Cutty and gave it a sniff. Drained it in two. Dark tracks down to the end and no white light. No hum on the tracks. Nothing. There was no moon at all. There was no train.

He inched forward and rode the clutch up and onto the raised tracks. Like it was the Jeep stepping up and not him. Rolled back and rocked it right up with his foot on the pedal and sat there. Right there. Well then. Well then. So.

Time for another Cutty, I'd say.

Cheers.

Then it happened. The red light flashing and the arms coming down in front and back. Coming down and the red light flashing. But there was no bright white eye. His eyes ripped to the other side. Nothing there either. There was no train no train no. But the arms were down and the red light. The arms were holding holding and he gunned it and he flew through the arm in front and the lights were still flashing and part of the arm was bouncing off the hood and the windshield and the back tires were spinning and he could hear the gravel spitting up into the tire wells and his foot was all the way down jammed to the floor and the bush and trees were thrown up bright in the headlights and he was turning and all the little Cutty bottles were sliding one after the other down the dashboard and onto the floor and he was on the long straight road now and there was no train no train no train and the other arm in the rear-view went back up no train and the red lights stopped flashing and there was no train and fuck fuck   fuck

&

This is what civilians must feel like in a war, Haven thought. Always vulnerable. Open. Waiting for the bombs. I've always felt this way. I don't know any other way to be.

&

Chase heard a cupboard door and thought that his mother was probably up and cooking again. He listened for a while to Haven breathing next to him and the sound of slippers in the kitchen. It was hot. You could hear the crickets and bullfrogs through the screen. He decided to get up. Maybe she'd bake something.

When he got to the end of the hall he could see her. She was under the light by the counter and she was in her underwear. She was leaning on the counter. Usually she wore her bathrobe. He wasn't sure now what to do.

'Mom?' he asked.

She looked over at him and her eyes were shadows under the light.

'Do you want a sandwich?' she asked.

'Sure.'

She patted the table and he went and sat in his chair. She sat down across from him and sat looking over his shoulder. She didn't say anything else. Chase looked at the little sparkles in the table and tried to chip one out with his thumbnail like he always did even though he knew they were part of the table and didn't come out. There were toast crumbs and he pushed those into a pile with his finger like a plow.

'Nothing makes it go away,' she said.

He could hear a truck go by on the highway.

And she was shaking her head and then she put her head down on the table.

'Maybe you should go to bed?' he asked.

But she didn't say anything back.

He put his head down on the table too but it was hard. Another truck went by and then a car. Then it was quiet. She was breathing and the clock over the sink was ticking. He put his arms under his head like a pillow.

&

It fell to Haven to identify the body. It fell to Haven. Didn't know why it couldn't wait till morning. No matter. Seen enough dead bodies under sheets.

'That's him,' she said. 'Yes.'

Could tell there were some horrible wounds to his neck the way the technician was holding the sheet tight to his chin. Holding the sheet tight to his chin, like she was just a normal person, not someone who'd been to med school. The matted blood in his hair that they'd cleaned up a bit.

Shaking then. She was on her knees then. She was to the floor then. She was sobbing. Tight to his chin, like he was in bed, like getting tucked in. Lots of dead bodies under sheets. She was a professional. Felt herself shaking uncontrollably. Clean white tiles. The lab technician's hands on her shoulders. *Now I lay me down. I pray the lord.* She'd been rock solid the whole drive to the hospital. White tiles on the floor. Hands steady on the wheel. She was going to throw up. *My soul to keep.* Dammit she was going to throw up.

Chase.

Now I have to go on.

There were a lot of questions. For the first time, there were a lot of answers. Ones that she didn't have to even think about. Ones that were true. And then there were tears finally. She couldn't stop them. There were fluorescent lights that made a humming sound when no one was talking. Men with notebooks. Ladies with juice and Kleenex. They came in and went out. There was a clock that ticked. Things felt very big. Things felt over. There were three sharp pencils lined up on the table. She was tired. What would happen now?

Sometimes they had Chase somewhere else and that was the hardest. It was hard when he was there too because he saw her cry and she never let him see her cry. If he saw her cry he would think something was wrong. Something was wrong. What would happen now?

A man had a file folder and it had pictures of the inside of the trailer. He didn't say how he got them. He asked them questions about different things. He asked Chase if his father ever hit him. Chase looked at Haven.

'Son, has your father ever hit you?' he asked again.

'Yes,' Haven said.

Yes he has.

&

there was that there was that and there was the other thing and the thing to do was not to think about it just to pray and not to think and it would all go away just in smoke like we all go away in smoke like in the movie and what was left which was nothing just nothing and that was all there was and behind the house there were bushes and they were digging down into the ground with cold rooty fingers in the little clumpy dirt and the worms and you just had to trust just had to trust that they wouldn't break break through the wall with their hard little roots grasping and grip down the wall to the bed and he wouldn't think about that and if he could just sleep then he wouldn't think think think at all wouldn't think at all just sleep just sleep

&

Chase remembered looking up at the sky at night and realizing that when he wanted to look at a star, it would disappear. Only when he shifted his gaze to one side could he see it again. Haven explained that it was an optical effect produced by the sensory dead zone at the centre of the retinal wall. She used words like *ganglia* and *neuro sensitivities* easily. She said the lay term was *a blind spot*. He couldn't help thinking that a few hundred years ago, before anyone had been able to explain away the vanishing of a distant sun, the effect had been magic, that up to a moment before mentioning the phenomenon to her it was still a sort of a magic to him and somewhere within her explanation the magic had disappeared.

&

He heard it. Like a file on your bones. Like someone walking down a long hallway in cold shoes. Like they didn't know where they were going, or what would be at the end.

You could tell when his dad was like that – you did whatever he said.

He heard it. Heard it. Heard it. Heard it.

He heard it. Louder and louder.

He saw it. Like one dead eye filmed over. Like a tunnel that would kill you. Like a star coming to explode you.

He saw it. He saw it. Closer and closer.

He felt it. Like black oil in his spine. Like night inside of him. There.

He felt it.

over and over and over and over and over and over and over and over and over and over

There.

Clickety clickety clickety clack.

Coming to kill you.

You stand there. Don't you move. Don't you flinch. Don't you move.

Daddy?
Don't move.
Don't.

&

Haven and her dad were the only ones home. There were tomatoes and bread so she was making tomato sandwiches. Her dad was watching hockey on TV and having a beer. There was only one beer in the house so he was drinking it slowly. Her mom would bring home more.

'Dad, do you want a tomato sandwich?' she asked.

'Sure,' he called out. 'No, do we have any meat loaf?'

'Just tomatoes,' she said.

'Sure, tomato.'

So she was cutting the tomato thin and the sharp knife slipped and she felt it go soft through her thumb and she thought before she looked down that it would be okay and then she did look down and her blood was all over the counter and on the tomato and mixing in with the water of the tomato juice and she grabbed her thumb with her other hand and held it tight and what could she do so he wouldn't know she could stop the bleeding if she held it tight and she could wash up the blood it would sound like she was washing the knife and he wouldn't know she could keep holding her thumb and she could bring him the sandwich and he would keep watching his hockey and wouldn't look at her or her stupid thumb and then she could go into the bathroom and have a better look and for now she could just hold it in her fist tight and use her other hand and then she looked down and the blood was coming out between her fingers and squeezing tighter didn't stop it and it hurt and then everything was loud and her mouth went dry and she was going down and the floor was coming up and she was big and heavy and going down cold and numb.

She was lying on the couch and the hockey was still on the TV coming into blue focus and the voices and her dad was sitting there on the edge of the couch looking at her. Her hand was wrapped up in a towel and there was a box of Band-Aids torn open on the floor. His beer was spilled on the floor. He'd spilled his beer. There was a blanket on her legs.

'There you go,' he said.

And she didn't know what to say.

'You're okay now,' he said and he rested his hand on her stomach.

'You're okay now,' he said again.

She couldn't remember her marriage. Looked at the pictures like it had all happened to someone else. Laughing suddenly. But no memory. No reason why.

Lined up. Lined up. Lined up like that on the dash. Line them up. Like that. On the dash. Line them up. Like that. Little bottles from the liquor store. Line them up. You could get little bottles. From the liquor store you could get them. They used them on the planes but you could get them regular. They were more expensive that way than the big bottles but they were little bottles the same as the big. Like they were shrunk down. You could look though the green glass like little binoculars. Line them up on the dashboard while you wait. There wasn't much of a dashboard in the Jeep but you could tip them against the windshield to balance

159

them. Snow sweeping past in the night. While I wait. I'm doing it at night. I'm back here at night. Like it used to be with my father. And I'm not afraid. I'm not afraid. I'm drunk. But I'm not afraid. I hear that train a-comin'.

I hear that train a-comin', it's comin' 'round the bend.

Line them up. Cutty with the green glass bottle and the yellow label and the white sailing ship. Cutty Sark. Called it Cutty. You could walk into a bar and say, 'Cutty, on the rocks, a double.'

It's good. It's very good. I'm not afraid.

&

Lucky would not sleep unless he had the lumberjack shirt to bury his nose in. He would flip the shirt with his nose until one of the rips settled gently over him. Haven tried to wash the blood from it but it would not come out, tried to throw it out but Lucky would drag it back from the trash.

I know he's gone for good, she thought. But Lucky is not sure. In the birch wood he searches, looks, fusses the dead leaves. He checks the chair, the carpet, the corners of the house. Looks up every time the door opens.

&

Haven was dead. Dead and gone at thirteen. It was very sad. The death of children was always so sad. And now she was dead.

She had been doing this for some time, imagining various ways of being dead and then playing them out in her mind and on the floor, or the bed, driveway, bathtub, the bottom of the stairs. She lay on the floor of her bedroom with one leg turned awkwardly to the side just as she had let herself fall – just as she imagined that she would fall if she had experienced a cerebral hemorrhage. An embolism, she told herself, I've had an embolism and nobody knows yet.

It was peaceful. She would let her mind wander and try to slow down the thoughts that ran through it. The dead don't think, she told herself, there's no time for idle thinking, she thought, I am dead. She often filled up with a sadness that seemed to embrace all of the suffering in the world. She imagined the suffering of all the lost, unseen or abandoned things: stuffed animals under beds, lost children in shopping malls.

She tried to imagine a massive amount of pain followed by nothing, as if in falling she had cracked her skull open on the corner of the coffee table and the void that followed freed her from the hot searing pain. A thousand stars in her head. Then all of them fading out. She imagined the sudden screech of car tires, then the pain, then a darkness.

Eventually she would tire of it and then she would watch TV with Chase or do her homework grudgingly. Sometimes she'd listen to the radio with Aunt Mary. Or she would crawl into the closet with a book and the flashlight and eventually lose herself under the weight of sleep, the dreams of the hanging clothes and the sounds of passing trains.

&

'Take him with you.'

'What?'

'When you go camping, take Lucky with you, then you won't be alone.'

Alone.

&

Like a postage stamp with a small frame around it, this sharp bright image in Haven's head. When she thought about it, which she did only when it was not possible to do otherwise, it was as if the image were surrounded by a void of black, a small, sharp, well-lit picture hovering in the emptiness of all that framed it like the flame of a candle: her parents in the tiny kitchen of the trailer, framed and glowing from the single light bulb, seen from down the dark tunnel of the small hall that led to the room she had shared with Chase. A single clear light in the dark. She was five. Yes.

Her mother placed gently in the kitchen chair, feet squarely on the floor, the rest of her body rising in a curve that swept down to hold her father, her father kneeling, his head in her lap. Her hand resting gently in his hair and then drawing up to her face and her eyes going then to the window and gazing out for a moment or staring at a reflection. Then her hand to her mouth and her eyes closing and her head shaking from side to side slowly for a moment, as if in disbelief. Haven had stretched to look out the window in her bedroom to see the car up on the front lawn, smoke puffing up out of the front of it like a series of ghosts.

It was almost all that she had of her mother, and more than she wanted of her father.

'No,' her mother had said softly, as if someone might hear. 'No ... no.'

&

This is what I know ...

'The way that she held herself. Up. Like I say, all the other girls were just there – your mother, she had a way of sitting. Being there like she meant it.'

They were at the kitchen table, just him and his dad.

'Like it meant something for her to be there – well, it meant something to me anyway. I watched her all that night. I was working helping the caller with the cards, I'd check the winners back to make sure they had the friggin' bingo.'

The smell of the dishwater. This paper lampshade with the light it threw on the plastic tabletop with the little flecks of metal. His father's beer. This square of window in the night.

'I'd work my way closer to her, then someone else would call a bingo. I'd have to move away.'

This is what I know.

'Move closer, move away … I don't know how many times I took a look at her card.'

Haven. This place. Those trees lined against the cold dark. It was gym again tomorrow.

'Even though she never called a friggin' bingo.'

This is what I know. He kind of wished his father would stop talking. But he also wished he'd keep going. He wished Haven and his mother would get home too.

My mother. My father. Haven. All that is inside my head.

'Closer, away … '

His father opened another beer. Dropped the cap onto the floor.

This is all that I know.

It happened. Like this. The lights went out and she. She drove. To his house. Where he lived. When he lived in the basement of that woman's house on Clothier. Would have been just around the time Ken left. Or she left him. Whichever. She drove.

All the lights were out everywhere. There was freezing rain and it was hard to see anything but she went there. Because. There was nowhere else she could think to go so she took April who was six then and she went. Knocked on the door down at the stairs in the back and then he was there with a flashlight looking ghostly. She had slid most of the way from the car, her arms wrapped around April holding her up.

On the way, a transformer at the top of a power line had been on fire and shooting sparks like bright fireworks across the street. She had driven through it like a waterfall, slid through it like the stars falling lightly. April's eyes big. Lucky going crazy in the back seat. His landlady couldn't stand dogs. Wouldn't let Chase keep Lucky overnight. She'd have to tonight.

'It's dark,' Haven said.

'I know. Come in.'

They sat at the little metal table in the kitchen and told stories for April in the dark. Chase turned out the flashlight to save the batteries and they sat talking and listening to the radio, which was saying that the power was out all over eastern Ontario and Quebec and parts of New York. After they stopped saying anything new on the radio, Chase turned it off and they sat talking for a while longer. Chase made hand shadows on the wall with the flashlight. Eventually it got cold.

'I don't know where Ken is,' Haven said suddenly.

'You should just stay here,' Chase told her.

So they did, the three of them curled up on the little bed, Chase behind her and April in front of her. They could hear sirens now and then. Chase rested his hand on Haven's shoulder. She held on to Chase's arm. The clack of the ice on the snow sounded like the end of the world. Haven sat up and looked out the basement window to the black mirror of the yard and the glass. She shifted April and lay back down facing Chase.

'Do you want me to sleep on the couch?' he asked.

'No,' she said.

She held him tighter. *If we stay like this*, Haven thought.

'No, it's all right,' she told him again.

If we stay like this, it will be all right … we will be okay.

If we stay like this, she told him with her body. Insistently with her body. Wrapping his and April's with her own. Convincing him. Like it all depended on right now.

If we stay like this …
we can stay like this
we can just stay like this.

drumming drumming drumming with your hands on the wheel and the falling snow your cold hands on the wheel plastic and the smell of the seats the smell of the Cutty everything cold the seats crack when you move the frost it keeps growing on the glass like angels would like angels would grow on the head of a pin he heard that once where was that you could find them on the head of a pin like you could find trolls under a bridge like you could find fairies in the garden if you looked up you could see him if you looked into the stained glass windows the frost on the window glass and you're drumming drumming drumming drumming drumming drumming drumming drumming drumming keeps your fingers warm and the snow like that have another drink look up into the snow like Christmas and it doesn't matter so much it doesn't matter so much does it? Stars disappearing.

And the creak of the jacket leather in the cold every time you take a drink or move your arm for anything and then the bell will ring and then the arms will come down red flashing eyes with their hoods and the train track picture sign like a grinning skull and then you'll cry like a baby like a baby and the red light flashing

and the bell ringing and the arms will come down and oh Christ
I'm sorry sorry I said I was sorry

arms will come down

I'm so sorry.

I said I was.

Arms coming down.

'Forchrissakel'llteachyou – don't move – don't be afraid!'

His father drunk. His father mad. Standing at the side of the
tracks. And the train coming.

Haven, there's a picture of Tom Thomson in this book I'm reading that I wish you could see. It's a photograph, black and white
of course, and he's standing on a little finger of land stretching out
into the water. It looks maybe like the ice has just gone out of the
lake, you can see some still floating by the edges of the canoes. He's
suspended out there like a bird on a branch gazing out into the
mid-horizon of the water and there's a dog with him – a jackknife
of a man, reflected, mirrored on the smooth water of the lake, and
this thin pencil of land with the two of them balanced at the end
of it and repeated upside down below – a long paintbrush of a man
and this ink dog at his feet. He's probably just thinking about what
he's going to have for breakfast but he's staring out at the water
and you know it could be Canoe Lake that he's looking at. That's
the lake he died in. Anyway, I wish you could see it. He's just looking out. It's a hell of a picture. It's dark here now and I'm going to
bed. I'll call you in the morning. It's a long message I know. I'm

okay.

Okay … I'll call you in the morning.

I'm okay now.

Bye.

The occasional truck. A car lost. There wasn't much came down the road at night. Empty headlights.

'Don't you flinch.'

'Don't you flinch.'

'Don't flinch.'

'Don't flinch.'

He tried not to. Tried not to when he was four. Tried not to at thirty-six. There were so many ways to come undone. No way to stay together.

Shoot him and strap him to the hood of the car like one of his fucking deer and drive him through town so all his buddies can see the trail of blood, the shattered bone and the matted hair. The open mouth and tongue lolling.

&

A dog wild through the cold arctic of the black night forest chimney trails scraping grey and still panting and heaving lungs with the cold whipping branches black branches on the blue star sky and free finally of the trees and across fields heavy with rolling snow red trailing tongue bounding through drifts and circling back a string of saliva trailing frozen silver from the turn of the head and then gone and then gone … over the hills and far away into the dark … to describe something as tragic, to say that something was tragic …

His dream of a black dog in the cold. It was him of course. He knew that. Dreamt it again and again.

&

Haven was so tired of studying. Luminol glows in a darkened room when it comes into contact with trace amounts of blood. Bright blue or green. Sprayed from a bottle, like Windex. Showed all the places where the pain was hidden.

&

'Haven, can you help me?'

'What are you trying to do?'

Chase was sitting at the kitchen table with his pencil and a ruler.

'Scalene triangles,' Chase said, putting his name at the top of his notebook page.

'I know how to make triangles,' their father said from the couch.

Chase looked at Haven.

'I can make you some triangles,' he said again, getting up from the couch and coming over to the table.

'They have to be scalene, though, Dad,' Haven said.

Chase could tell that she was tensing her body and getting ready to move quickly.

'Okay, whatever,' he said and he sat down next to Chase and took the pencil.

'Scalene, praline, Plasticine … '

He started making triangles at the top of the page and kept doing the same kind over and over. They weren't scalene.

Chase looked at Haven again. She told him *no* with her eyes.

'Those are good, Dad,' she said.

'Damned straight. Give me that ruler.' He took the ruler and kept making the triangles.

Haven looked at Chase and moved him away from the table with her eyes.

'Thanks for helping, Dad,' she said, pulling Chase back and into the bedroom and closing the door.

'Don't go back out there,' she said.

She knew when to hide. Could always tell when to get away.

They stayed at the Harts' house until Aunt Mary was there and ready to take them. Carol said she was coming from Ireland and it would take several weeks. The Harts lived in the country and had some cows in an old barn. The house smelled like soup. Everyone got up really early. There was no liquor in the house as far as Haven could tell. People just drank milk and water. The floor in the living room was linoleum same as the kitchen. They watched *Jeopardy!* on TV and called out the answers. They played a game called Parcheesi. Went to bed early.

It took longer than Carol said for Mary to come so they had to start going to school. They put Chase in the same class as Haven even though it wasn't his grade. They sat together. They said prayers every morning. Kids let them play games at recess. For lunch they had ham or peanut butter sandwiches wrapped in wax paper. Apples. Ritz crackers and cheese. They had pickled beets. They threw those out. They each had a Thermos that kept their milk cold and fit into a lunchbox. Haven's was the Partridge Family. Chase had the Monkees.

But Haven couldn't sleep. Lay awake and listened to the wind. Chase breathing.

Foot on the gas. Head in the stars above and not so much winning as not losing so much anymore. And it was good. For a little while. But it always changed. Always. Always. Out of reach. Always split apart. Nothing he could do to stop it.

&

Burnt and scorched clothing may or may not be noted on the body. In some instances a leaf-like pattern of skin mottling may be seen. Metal objects on the body or nearby may display a welded appearance or demonstrate magnetic qualities. Extremely high voltages are likely to have been expressed in a lightning strike that will have produced a 'blast effect' – a blast wave produced by the discharge of electricity.

Haven read of cases where a bobby pin in a pocket was twisted in an arc and the body showed no marks at all.

High-voltage electrical cables are commonly found near railway lines and can cause accidental death. The high voltages may propel the body some distance and visibly char the skin. The development of rigor mortis may be accelerated in electrocution fatalities.

Slowly turning the pages. Looking for the answers she needed. There was always another test.

Place victim on back. Turn face to one side to allow water to drain from mouth. Facing victim, kneel astride victim's hips. With one of your hands on top of the other, place the heel of your bottom hand on the upper abdomen below the rib cage and above the navel. Use your body weight to press into the victim's upper abdomen with a quick upward thrust. Repeat until water no longer flows from the mouth.

Haven put her head down. Just for a minute. Then she'd study more.

'Tell me about my father,' Haven said, like a command rather than a question.

'I don't know anything to tell,' Mary replied, scraping margarine onto a slice of bread.

'You must know something.'

'I know he's dead.'

'Before that.'

Mary took two slices of deli meat and cut into a tomato, sliding it onto the bread and licking the back of her thumb.

'Will April eat this for her lunch?' she asked.

'Yes. What else do you know?'

'Nothing you don't. I know he worked for a while, he pumped gas and he drove a truck, then he just went wrong and he took my sister with him … and I got you. So everybody gets something in this life.'

'What did my father get?'

Mary thought for a moment. 'Drunk.'

Their mother wanted a family picture for Christmas, so they had to drive to Sears in Ottawa one night to get it taken. Everybody had to take turns in the bathroom and then get dressed up in the clothes she said. Haven had to wear the dress. There was even a necktie for Chase. He could tell that his father didn't want to go.

'You know it's snowing,' he called from the kitchen table where he sat with a beer he'd just opened, flipping the cap into the trash. Red Cap, Chase knew.

His mother wasn't paying attention; she was in their bedroom helping Haven with her hair. Chase went in to watch. He sat on the bed.

'It's December, it's supposed to snow,' she called back.

You could never tell whether something was going to be a fight or not. Not until it already was. He looked at Haven. Her face didn't tell him anything yet.

'It could be worse on the way back – that's all I'm saying,' his father complained.

His mother took a bobby pin from her mouth. 'That's not all you're saying,' she said under her breath so that only Haven and Chase could hear her.

'What?'

She put her hands on her hips and looked at Haven in the mirror. 'It won't be worse on the way back,' she said louder.

She brushed Haven's bangs back with a finger. 'We'll stop at the chip wagon,' she added.

Chase could tell she was bargaining with him. He heard another beer snap open.

'Go get your father to help you with your tie,' she told Chase and she winked at him.

Chase looked at Haven. Haven nodded, a nod so small only he could see it. She nodded with her eyes.

Chase looked at the red shining tie in his hands. It was a clip-on. He didn't need much help.

He walked slowly out into the hallway carrying the tie like a small dead animal. His father was using a dishcloth to polish his shoes and he looked up when Chase walked in. Chase didn't say anything, just went over to the table and showed his father the tie. His father looked at him.

Then he made a sound with his tongue against his cheek, 'Tchk,' and he winked too.

And he took the tie from Chase and looked at it. Then he looked at Chase.

'Chip wagon,' he said. Then he said, 'Extra salt.'

He always ordered extra salt and so did Chase. His father always said extra salt to the man in the wagon like he was trying to cheat people on the salt and Chase's father knew what he was up to.

'Follow me,' he said and Chase followed him down the hall.

They passed the door where his mother was pulling at Haven's dress like she was trying to make it fit the right way. Haven looked at him. She was seeing if it was okay. But he didn't really know.

He followed his father into his parents' bedroom. It was somewhere they didn't usually go. The bed was made. Usually through the door on the way from the bathroom you could see that the bed wasn't made.

His father opened the closet door where there was a fulllength mirror screwed to the back.

His father was wearing a white shirt and black pants. The black belt with the silver buckle. The edges of his sleeves were fuzzy. He put his beer down on the dresser.

'C'mere,' he said.

Chase went where he showed with his hands, standing in front of him facing the mirror. Suddenly he had a bad feeling about what would happen.

His father's big hands slid in front of him with the tie and pulled at his collar then pushed the tab in and snapped it shut. His father kneeled down behind him and looked over his shoulder into the mirror. He could feel his father's breath on the side of his face.

'Stand still,' his father whispered.

Chase went cold.

Then his father smiled, stood and ruffled Chase's hair.

'Extra salt,' he said and he left the room.

Left Chase staring into the mirror. Years later he looked at the picture. Still had the same expression on his face.

Chase sat and looked at the little robot that sat on his desk holding down a stack of drawings of trains. He had bought it in a store in Toronto and had kept it on his desk ever since. He had gotten rid of most of the things from Toronto because they reminded him of Ivy. But he kept the robot. It was about four inches tall and painted grey with white and red gears and electrodes painted where its belly would be if it wasn't a robot and had a belly. Its feet were large and red like a clown's and when you wound it with a key it clattered and shook and walked along the top of the desk or on the floor. There were little dials on its chest and rivets painted all around the outside of its torso. It had a spring attached to the top of its head that was supposed to look like an antenna. Chase noticed for the first time its expression: a long straight grille of a mouth with straight white teeth wrapped in red painted lips and two large round white eyes that made it look as if the robot had drunk way too much coffee. It was a harried expression, as if the robot had been unnerved by something. Arms like wrenches that hung by its side and dangled uselessly when it moved. Chase took it outside in the dark and beat it with a hammer until it was completely flat and in pieces. The pieces he took back inside and kept on the desk for a few days until he got around to guiltily throwing them into the garbage. Shattered.

Teachers collected pictures. At least she did. A sad drawer full of them. Underneath the broken staplers and the hockey cards. When she worked late at report-card time sometimes she took them out. Mostly class pictures. Teachers knew. You could look at each picture and you could tell. You could tell which kids went home to no supper. And you could tell which were confused by parents that were supposed to be like all the others but weren't. All of us, she thought, hurrying after things that just hold us.

The plaster at the bottom of the wall had the texture of day-old cake and Haven would lie curled on the closet floor at night and dig at it softly with a spoon. Sometimes she thought it felt like carving through flesh to splintery wooden bones and at others it was more like digging through earth to shifting rock. She slept with slivers of the house slipped beneath her nails. She woke with the scent of plaster on the back of her tongue. She kept digging. It wasn't so much that she thought there was anything there to find – she was fourteen, she knew there was nothing to find. The books were just books. This was just this. Life wasn't easy, but it was easier than it had been. There was no counting the ways she was grateful – no way to count the number of ways in which she was disappointed. Not to let your weaknesses define you, Haven thought, is the thing.

April was getting snippy more and more often. There were times that Haven was just too tired to deal with it. It was part of being eleven. It was part of growing up. Of course she was going to have some resentment. She was going to be angry at her father for leaving. And she was going to take it out on Haven. All the books said so and they said to just ignore it. April had just told her to shut up and was shoving her chair from the table but was stopped by the presence of Mary at her elbow with a plate of cookies.

'Have a cookie,' Mary said simply.

'No,' April said, still making to get up. 'Thanks,' she added, sensing that it was not a good time to be rude to her great-aunt.

Mary rested her hand very lightly on April's shoulder.

'Have one,' she said. 'Your mother made them for you because she loves you more than anything and she can't bear to see you suffering at all. Which if you were a more considerate daughter and spent more time thinking about your mother ... ' She paused as April lowered to her seat once more. 'You wouldn't be so anxious to make such a big performance.' She paused once more.

'I can speak to you like this because I'm old and because I'm your great-aunt and I might as well be your grandmother and I'm … colourful … and because I love you. Now sit back down and have a cookie.' She looked over at Haven and smiled. 'They're a little doughy but they're fresh from the oven.'

Haven smiled back.

'About as fresh from the oven as you are, April,' Mary added, 'so don't be in such a hurry to be a big grown-up girl. There's more to it than just being a bitch.'

'Mary!' Haven interjected.

Mary's hand was still resting carefully on April's shoulder next to April's now chalk-white face.

'I'd throw myself in front of a bus for you, April, you know that. Now have a cookie.'

April took a cookie and sat still. Mary put the plate on the table.

'I'll get the milk.'

There was silence.

Haven watched an old movie with April, curled into one elongated ball on the couch, arms and legs wrapped up together in sweaters and blankets. Cookies and milk and the healing of the world. *You have to love your wounds*, Mary had told her, *or they will never heal.*

176

One night when they were driving, Chase saw a little boy with a lot of blond hair and a T-shirt walking by the side of the road. It was late for a boy to be out alone. But he looks happy, Chase thought.

Like nothing bad had ever happened to him.

Chase came home after school once and found his father in the driveway. The cedar hedge by the side of the trailer was gone. His father had it tied up in sections lined along the driveway with a sign on each that said $10. The signs were written in green and red magic marker on cut-up pieces of cardboard.

There was even a string of Christmas lights strung overhead. His father was wearing big boots and his plaid hunting coat. He had cut sections of string to help people tie the sections of hedge onto the tops of their cars. Was that hot chocolate on the hot plate by the door?

'Is that hot chocolate?'

'Want some?'

He had the tin tool box cleaned out and sitting on a table for the money.

'Sure.'

Chase thought about his father searching through the house trying to find one red marker and one green marker. Looked at the brown holes where the hedge had been.

Every night Chase would fall asleep with a can of Dr. Pepper on the nightstand so he'd know where it was in the morning. A mouth like ashes.

&

Tell me that I'm beautiful with your eyes, she was thinking. Just with your eyes, Ken, not a card from the drugstore or with words. Words mean nothing ... tell me with your eyes. With your hands. Tell me we will always be like this. Lie to me.

&

For a time he buried model trains. There was a little store about ten minutes away in Merrickville and after he bought the Jeep he would drive there once a week and buy a train car – there was a bin with old ones that nobody really wanted for half price. He wanted them all to be engines but the engines were all really expensive because they had electric motors in them. He would take each car home and at night he would bury them in little holes he dug in the backyard behind the house where he rented the basement. He had to do it at night so nobody would know. Sometimes he would hear the sound of the train whistle while he was digging. Those were the best ones. He would mark each little grave with crossed twigs. The landlady never worked in the garden and it was all overgrown with weeds so he didn't feel guilty about disturbing anything – he knew they wouldn't be found until years later and then whoever came across them would just think that it was the work of children, or that there had been a particularly careless child always leaving toys outside. He would have kept on doing it – it was a very peaceful thing to do and he enjoyed it – except that one night, halfway through filling dirt back over the top of a passenger car, he suddenly realized that what he was doing was strange. A part of him realized that. One of the things he had to do at night. So no one would know. No one would.

&

It was news to Haven that her mother had once pulled a drowning man from a frozen river.

'Katherine would have been fifteen then. I would have been nine,' Mary told her while setting out the cups and saucers.

They had been by a river in winter, Mary didn't exactly remember why – something to do with their father's work. He sometimes took them with him travelling through the countryside taking orders for farm equipment. It was late and getting dark but he had one more stop. He had gone off with the farmer to the barns and the two of them, Mary and Haven's mother, had wandered down by the river.

'It wasn't often we saw a river,' Mary said. 'And we saw the poor lad, walking on the ice with a bundle of sticks over his shoulder. The whole river wasn't frozen over, you see, just the edges where he was walking, and we were young, we didn't know you shouldn't be walking on ice like that, until he went down. Like a piece of toast into a toaster, just slow and straight and then he cried out. Your mother grabbed me by the shoulders and she told me to stay put no matter what happened and then she left me there, by the shore … '

Her mother had run out onto the ice, tripped once and fallen face first into the snow. She recovered herself and proceeded more carefully, slowly, to the thrashing man. Mary remembered her inching her way towards the edge of the water.

'She said his face was already blue from the cold.'

She grasped at him. Grasped at the sticks he'd been carrying on his back. Made her fingers work with no feeling in them.

'I don't know how she did it, the slip of a thing she was. I ran then to get Dad.'

'I was scared to death. By the time I got back with Dad she had the man onto the ice and she was straddling him. I don't know how she knew what to do – fifteen-year-old girl. This would've been 1947, don't think anyone had ever heard of the Heimlich manoeuvre, or artificial respiration … '

Mary buttered some bread and took the kettle off the stove. Haven took a deep breath and let it out. Mary looked down at her.

'Too clever by half,' she said.

Haven tried to picture her mother doing all of that. Mary poured the milk.

'Didn't work, though. By that time he was dead. Shock got 'im, likely.'

Haven sat looking at Mary.

'Well,' Mary said, 'she tried.'

Haven saw the man's blue face, staring up into the cold.

The Jeep kept dying on the road. It was easy to fix. The positive cable to the battery had rusted right out of its clamp so you just had to pull over to the side and jam it back in. The rattling of the engine worked it loose. You jammed it back in again. He could afford to have it fixed properly. It wouldn't be much. He could just buy a new clamp and a cable at Canadian Tire. But he liked being by the side of the road and knowing what to do to fix it. The bugs around his head. The sun on his hands. Or at night in the dark with headlights going by. This secret knowledge of what to do.

'Amazing Grace.'

The choir had just learned it for the monthly mass in the high school auditorium. She preferred the church like in the old school but it was nice in the auditorium too. She liked the folding seats and the way voices carried in the darkness. The way the noise of the audience died down when they came out to sing. She liked the plaid skirt and the crisp white top. When she was a kid she had never worn anything so clean that it was crisp. It had taken her a while to get used to wearing something new each day. The choir gave recitals too, sometimes at assemblies and sometimes in the evening for parent things, and Mary went to the things in the evenings. She never said much but she was always there. Once when they were driving home, Mary said, 'Nice voices.'

There was a time that the choir had gone to Kingston for a big concert and the school bus hadn't left to come back to Ottawa until after nine o'clock. When they started out, people had been talking and there was the general school-bus noise but it had been a long day and people settled down fairly quickly. Haven stared out past her own face at the farms and fields and the white houses and grey fences sliding silently past in the dark. She wasn't sure how it started, somewhere from the back of her throat and then she was singing it softly, breathing it to the window, and a little louder and a little louder. Amazing grace, how sweet the sound. And then some of the others joined in and then most of the bus except for the ones who were asleep and they went through the song about five times. When they got off at the school the bus driver said, 'That was lovely ... just lovely.'

And everybody was really quiet because they knew.

It had been.

And it had been the first time that she saw how God worked.

Chase loved Monday nights because usually on Mondays they had cereal for dinner, when there was cereal, and then they could stay up to watch *Rowan and Martin's Laugh-In*.

'Do you know what you'd do?'

'What?'

'If you were to kill yourself, like you say – do you know how you'd do it?'

'Not really.'

He hadn't given it much thought. Didn't think it would be that complicated.

'Let's go to the other world,' she would say to herself.

'Okay,' she would answer, 'let's.'

She was reading a book from the school library about a kid named Milo who went into his closet and came out the other side and ended up in another world where everything was magical and different and he had a little car he could drive around and he had adventures with numbers that could talk and strange creatures. She had been reading the book for a long time and she couldn't take it back now because there would be a fine and she had no money and she was worried that they wouldn't let her take it out again. She liked reading it so much that she was afraid now to finish it so every time that she got close to the end she would turn back to the beginning and start again.

She would sit behind the sliding door in the tiny closet in their room in the trailer with the book and a flashlight, every so often reaching out to test the panelling of the wall to see if it had given away to a magical world.

'Are you ever coming out?' Chase would complain from their bed.

'No. Go to sleep.'

Often she would fall asleep curled in among the shoes, the flashlight shadowing the empty sleeves reaching down to touch her head, the flashlight tilting across the piles of shoes and shining off the unmoving panelling.

I don't know what to do.
   I don't know what to do.
   And I don't know what to do.
   Haven, I don't know what
   to do. Now.
   His kind of strength: leaving.

'You can leave me if you want,' she had said several times to Ken, the last of them in the car in the rain as they backed out of the driveway, his neck craning to grasp a look out over his shoulder, leaves falling from the trees in the dark, his hand pulling at the wheel. But she never thought that he would.

&

She heard at school once some of the kids saying that any slivers that were not removed right away would eventually find their way to your heart and kill you and she'd had this image of all the

unclaimed shards of wood in her bloodstream like a log jam
making its inexorable way to the centre of her chest. They would
slowly make their way to her heart, which would burst like a ripe
tomato inside her and she would die. She pictured it in the darkness. Chase shaking her while she clutched at her chest. No
breath. There was no way out. It was not yet dawn. When there
was enough light out it would be safe to get up.

&

'Ms. O'Donnell? Haven O'Donnell? I'm sorry, did I wake you?'
    'No, no, no … I was just … ' She rolled over and dragged a
hand through her hair and searched the night table for a barrette,
struggling to shake off the sleep. Whoever this was couldn't see
her over the phone – her fingers stopped searching.
    It's a nurse, it's a hospital. Chase.
    It was 1:53 in the morning.
    'Yes?'
    'I've been asked to contact you about your brother.'
    'Is he … '
    But she knew.

&

'Did you ever think about all the dead people in the world,' Ivy
asked him once, 'and how many graves there are? It's not near
enough of them for all the dead people. Where do you think
they're putting them all?'
    'I don't know.'
    He turned out the light. Didn't sleep.

184

Haven would sleepwalk with the intent of making things right. A little girl in the dark. Sightlessly she would make her way to the kitchen slowly down the carpeted hall, sidestepping or shuffling through the clothes and the debris of lives lived in the dark. Her hands would find their way into the cupboards and she would meticulously spread plates and cutlery across the surface of the table. Her fingers, like the fingers of the blind, roaming over the hidden language of the surfaces, testing the weights and textures against her skin. Forks here ... knives ... here. here. She would sit finally before it all, in her dream-straightened mind everything lined just as it should be. She would sit with satisfaction and fold her hands carefully before herself.

'Wake up, Haven,' Chase would tell her, wiping his eyes in the darkness, 'you've made a mess again ... '

Sometime after they moved she started sleeping through the night.

She knew what had happened and she knew what would happen next. She stood in the hallway near the office, not too close, and she watched the people come and go. Once the crowd thinned, she knew, she would be identifiable: the girl whose parents did not pick her up, the girl still wearing the costume wings from the pageant and standing by the frozen windows, the forgotten girl. She had to become invisible before she became obvious. She would be asked to sit at the office and a teacher would look in a big binder for her phone number and they would phone and they would be looking at the clock and waiting for an answer and then they would say, 'It says this number's not in service, Haven ... Is there a new number?'

And Haven would say, 'We got a new phone, but it's a different number, it's one of those new phones. I don't know the number yet.'

She slipped out the front door with a family that was laughing and talking about the show: the snow looked so real, the singing was wonderful, it's almost Christmas. She disappeared.

It's almost Christmas.

She was dressed as an angel with a shimmering gown and with wings made from a wire hanger and sparkling tissue paper. It was so cold that the insides of your nose stiffened on contact with the air and glued themselves together. One foot in front of the other, she thought, and then we're home. Cold. When you're cold you're cold, nothing to do about it. She pulled her gown tighter around herself and concentrated on her walking. Cars slid by on the crunching snow, like Styrofoam, she thought, all the air frozen out of it.

She headed down the street towards the hotel at the corner where a slim string of Christmas lights hung blandly in the window, reflecting a pale pink and yellow light into the carved tire ruts and footprints. Haven turned left and made her way past the Giant Tiger mall and the IGA. Places were closing now, only a few cars left in the parking lots and one or two shoppers stepping through drifts, with their arms filled with bags.

At the Beer Store she knew she was fifty-seven mailboxes from home and she turned into the Mac's parking lot and went inside to get warm for a while. When her feet started to tingle and get feeling again she wished that she had gone back to the classroom to get her coat and boots, but it was too late now, she thought, the school would probably be locked up. There was a lady in the store looking at her wings, then at the magazines and then back at her wings, so Haven left and started to walk towards the liquor store through the clouds of exhaust at the gas bar. She realized that it was the cold that was making the fumes so visible, the five or six cars creating a cloud close to the ground that she swirled through in her gown. By the time she got to the edge of the lot and stopped to cross the street she was shaking, and she held her elbows in tight to her sides to look both ways. Since she had been in the store it had started to snow, and the passing headlights haloed small solar systems of flakes swirling and tunnelling them down to the frozen ground.

Haven crossed the street and climbed over the snowbank at the edge of the road. Ahead she could see the Christmas tree gleaming on top of the liquor store. She would not be allowed to go into the liquor store, she knew, then it was the police station, she couldn't go there, then the gas station where they sold chocolate bars. She would be able to warm up again there. She kept walking.

Chase had this dream where he was on a rock beach with Ivy and they were walking. She was wearing white shorts and her red Roots sweatshirt. They were barefoot on the rocks, which were polished smooth by the water. Her hair was pulled back from her face. There was a spit of land where the rocks were piled high and he climbed up and reached back to give her his hand and he pulled her up. She was always smiling. Sometimes in the dream it was Haven. He was saving her. He was pulling her up.

When you're drinking you're running. And when you run you fall. The pattern on the wallpaper flipping and flipping like a film

187

caught in the gate. Eyes wildly trying to focus. And not. And not. It was all oysters, Chase thought, and no pearls.

&

Ivy's small body pale in the cold moonlight arching above him as she strained against him. And his heart raging.

&

Haven's eyes hurt. The linoleum was too bright. For old linoleum it was too bright – maybe it was the big flat fluorescent lights that hung suspended from the ceiling like waffles, maybe it was just that she was tired, but something was making her eyes hurt. Sitting in the only clothes they had, the ones they'd been wearing when they took the car. Through the window the moon was hanging full like a hole in the sky ... like somewhere to escape.

She could see herself reflected in the glass, her thin legs and her ridiculous sweater sitting in this plywood chair. Sitting next to Chase who was looking up to the front of the room where a woman wearing a Santa hat was playing the piano and trying to get people to sing 'Jingle Bells.' She watched Chase's mouth forming the words: 'laughing all the way, ha, ha, ha,' each *ha* a black hole in the glass. The woman was standing now and clapping her hands in front of her, the piano forgotten and her heavy shoes sliding one to the other on the floor in time. There were boxes of doughnuts on the table and paper cups of Kool-Aid. Hanging streamers with little paper Santas suspended from them. On the long table a centrepiece Santa that folded out to reveal a puffy tissue-paper belly. *No way*, Haven thought, *could this be worse.* The woman willing, forcing, the children to be excited.

'I think I can hear something … I think he's coming down the hall!'

I did not risk our lives for this crap.

There was a skinny boy wearing a toque – not much older than she was but he had a tattoo – he wore jeans and a green T-shirt that said Byward Lumber on it. His hair fringed out from under the toque. He had been walking around and helping the little kids with their Kool-Aid and doughnuts. The tattoo was on his forearm – a cross with rays of light coming out from it. Eventually he sat down next to her and looked at her, then looked away.

She put her arm around Chase. Her other hand held the book about the children and the closet. She ran her fingers over the surface of the leather cover. It was a piece of what was normal.

Haven noticed the small piece of paper amidst the general clutter of April's floor. It was like the thousands of scraps she had picked up when April was little. Brightly coloured, doodled drawings in marker and crayon. Rabbits, monsters, rainbows, hearts.

She hadn't noticed one in years and wondered where it had come from. It was really just the torn corner of a drawing. Maybe a drawing. Turquoise marker scribbles. Not the type of thing she usually saw now that April was a teenager. Something about picking up the underwear of your child when she was a teenager was so much less endearing than it had been when she was a child.

Haven rested against the door frame and watched April sleeping in the moonlight of the blinds. There was a science textbook on the bed next to her and a magazine. And tomorrow I will tell you that your great-aunt has died. I will shock and surprise you with the news that your great-aunt Mary has died. Confused and not remembering anyone in her life. But I will try to tell you in a way that makes sense and that does not hurt you unnecessarily. I will tell you in the awkward language of mother and teenager that has grown between us lately. I will try to tell you through that language of echoes. I will try to hold you as I tell you.

'Mary has died,' I will say.

She is gone.

She looked down at April's face in the darkness. Cleared the hair from her forehead. Read her T-shirt: 'This Is The Way That It Is.' Which was the name of a band or a CD, Haven knew that. The words stretched across her fourteen-year-old breasts. Haven still surprised that there were breasts there to stretch words. Slowly she crept down onto the bed behind April and rested one arm across her body.

We will, all of us, she thought, be forgiven. For everything we've done. And everything that we haven't. This is the way that it is. And I'm going to keep you safe. Somebody in this family ought to be safe. Someone deserves to be safe.

She went past the car dealer's with the swinging line of bright lights hanging in the snow. It seemed like forever now since the concert had ended and she had started this walk. The snow swept to one spot in front of her face and then stopped in the middle of the twisting wind and swung another way. It began to stick to her eyelashes, which began to stick to each other. At the lights she turned the corner and made her way slowly past the police station. Briefly she imagined a police officer in a big coat coming out and calling to her and then wrapping her in a blanket and bringing her inside where there was a real Christmas tree and hot chocolate. That was stupid, she knew, there wouldn't be a Christmas tree in a police station. Policemen didn't believe in Santa Claus.

They didn't drink hot chocolate; they'd have those Styrofoam cups of coffee with the little plastic lids and they'd all stand around drinking and looking at her in her wings and her blanket and they'd ask her a lot of questions and then she wouldn't get home and Chase would be alone. When she got to the gas station that sold chocolate bars she kept going. She didn't have any money for chocolate bars and she wanted to get home now. She couldn't feel her feet except for her toes, which felt like ice, and her nose, which felt the same. She could tell they were there only because of how cold they were. Everything else she couldn't really tell at all except for when she shivered and then she could feel the bones in her like sticks rattling against each other and she thought of her skeleton walking like that through the snow and then she thought that maybe it hadn't been such a good idea to leave the school. Maybe it would have been better for someone to call and have her father swear and then show up at the school drunk and then the police gathering around anyway because the principal or a teacher would call them and all the questions and then maybe it would just all be over and she wouldn't have to try so hard. She sat down finally and looked up into the maze of snow and into the close and holy night and she wondered what would happen next. It was almost Christmas.

When the woman who had seen her in Mac's found her she had made it to the bridge over the highway and had sat down again in a snowbank to rest. The woman had driven past the same spot twice before seeing her there in the dark, slowly being wrapped in the falling snow, her face almost covered in the white.

The woman almost decided just to drive ahead home with her can of gravy when she came out of the store and didn't see Haven at the corner because of the truck blocking her. At first she turned the other way towards her house but slowed, peering through the snow at the sidewalk, and then turned around at the mall and drove back the other way, doubling back a couple of times and finally spotting her by the side of the bridge. It had been the wings that had kept her looking.

&

'Mom?'

And Haven had that immediate parental urge to deny that anything was wrong, to wipe her eyes and to protect, but there had been no use – she was sitting in a pile of laundry with the tears streaming down her face and she just reached out for April and held her there and they cried together finally, Haven holding this smaller version of herself and speaking of Chase and the bear and what had happened, that they were still a family, that they would just have to learn to be this new thing now, the two of them with the same wound, two who had both lost something that morning in a forest. She stroked April's hair, pulling her in and sheltering her from the things that would make clear to her the pain of the world. It's going to be okay.

'It's going to be okay.' She said it again. When she knew that this was a mother's lie to hold against the darkness.

At night Haven would study her face in the mirror. She knew the look of people who had been beaten down by their lives, had seen people whose lives had run over them like an eighteen-wheeler and left them dazed. A couple of weeks earlier she had been driving home from the school and had seen a couple sitting by a sad-looking little garage sale, their lives spread out over the lawn like a bazaar: little macramé hand towels and plastic salt and pepper shakers, used car mats … Why would anyone buy used car mats, she wondered, everyone already owned used car mats. And the looks on their faces as they sat by a plastic table smoking in front of a house crying out for paint, the man getting up to rearrange some drinking glasses and Tupperware pitchers and pulling at his belt, the shine on the seat of his pants, the woman watching him with little interest and then stubbing out her smoke on the leg of her chair, the looks on their faces as if they had been beaten with hammers and were just too stubborn to lie down and admit that it was over.

She pulled on her cheeks in the mirror and made faces. She thought it was good that she made faces – to stare lifeless into the mirror would be bad, to make faces, that was ... What was it? Childlike. There was an optimism in that, surely, to stick out your tongue at yourself, there was some merit in that and there was some hope, there was more than just the lying down and the letting go of things. Surely it was good that she continued to brush her teeth and hair and maintain an interest in her personal appearance. Surely her face would not keep that beaten look she thought it had begun to take on and that she could not see provided she continued to make the faces in the mirror. Big eyes. Little eyes. Scrunched nose. Squinty eyes. This is what I look like when I'm about to throw up. Big cheeks. This is what I would look like if I were screaming, but I'm not.

I haven't been. I won't. Remember that time you read in the paper about how to make strawberry ice cream – you made some with April and the two of you sat at the kitchen table and ate all of it?

Chase?

How you used to fold little pieces of paper under the bridge of your sunglasses so your nose would not get sunburnt because you burn easily and I'd ask you why you didn't just buy the glasses that have a plastic shield to cover the nose and you'd say are you kidding then I'd look like an idiot. And Lucky won't sleep without that damned bloody shirt.

&

'No,' she said.

She held him tighter and she looked into his eyes for a moment. *If we stay like this*, Haven thought.

'No, it's all right,' she told him again.

If we stay like this, it will be all right … we will be okay.
If we stay like this …
we can stay like this.

&

I would still love you, she thought. If you were three birds or a leaf in the trees. A breath. If you were still here. I could still love you like that. Like a poem. Like all the sorrow and joy in the world. Like all the good things in the world. Like this. Like I do. If you were here.

She was at the small shrine she had built in the park. April knelt beside her. It was nice to see her giving her full attention to this. Nice to see her taking it in. And giving something.

Haven lit one of the small candles and watched the thin blue light flicker through the glass. And now he's okay, she thought.

April lit the second candle carefully.

Finally, he's okay, Haven thought.

It wasn't all that she wanted.

But it was enough.

She watched the cold blue flames flicker through the warped glass. Two clear lights in the dark. Eventually they would go out. But by then she would be gone.

We all get something, she thought.

No one is alone. Not really.

194

Then she was gone down the blue highway and out of the park following her headlights, under the black shadows and the big wood archway. April was already asleep beside her. Then there was the highway and the trees and then there was the great big empty sky. Haven kept her eyes forward.

Acknowledgements

My thanks go to all those who've helped this book in one way or another:

my mother, for reading so many books to me when
  I was young
Alana Wilcox, you are a marvel
Evan Munday, Christina Palassio, Stan Bevington
  and all at the remarkable Coach House

and

Beth Follett
Mary Newberry
Martha Magor
Janie Yoon
rob mclennan
Rhonda Douglas
Emily Schultz
Mike Crossan
John W. MacDonald
Tara
Taylor
Michaela
Timothy Findley
Kin Platt
Nicholas Hoare Books, Ottawa
Dr. Paula Norman
E.S.
Terry's Automotive, for getting the Jeep back
  on the road when it rolled

and

all who've helped to get the wheels back on the blacktop
these many times … it's not how many times you get
knocked down, it's how many times you get back up.

Guides

Williams, David J.,and Anthony J. Ansford, David S. Priday, Alex S. Forrest. *Forensic Pathology.* Edinburgh: Churchill Livingston, an imprint of Harcourt Publishers, 1998.

Strauss, Claudia J. *Talking to Alzheimer's.* Oakland, CA: New Harbinger Publications, 2001.

About the Author

Michael Blouin has been the recipient of the Diana Brebner Prize for Poetry from *Arc, Canada's National Poetry Magazine,* as well as the Lillian I. Found Prize for Poetry from Carleton University, and his work has been shortlisted for a National Magazine Award. He is the author of the collection of poetry *I'm not going to lie to you* (Pedlar, 2007), which was a finalist for the Lampman Scott Award and longlisted for a ReLit Award. He resides in Oxford Mills, a rural community near Ottawa.

Typeset in Adobe Garamond
Printed and bound at the Coach House on bpNichol Lane, 2008

Edited and designed by Alana Wilcox
Author photo by Tara Rutherford-Blouin

Coach House Books
401 Huron Street on bpNichol Lane
Toronto, Ontario M5S 2G5
Canada

416 979 2217
800 367 6360

mail@chbooks.com
www.chbooks.com